To Jim

May 26th 1982

The Maharajah and Other Stories

THE MAHARAJAH & OTHER STORIES
T. H. WHITE

Selected and with an introduction
by Kurth Sprague

G. P. Putnam's Sons
New York

First American Edition 1981

First published in 1981 in Great Britain by
Macdonald • London and Sydney

Library of Congress Cataloging in Publication Data

White, T. H. (Terence Hanbury), 1906–1964.
   The maharajah, and other stories.

   Contents: The maharajah—A sharp attack of some-
thing or other—The spaniel earl—[etc.]
   1.   Fantastic fiction, English.   I.   Sprague, Kurth.
II.   Title.
PR6045.H2M3   1981   823'.912   81-5923
ISBN 0-399-12650-3   AACR2

Contents

Introduction

He was viewed by one of his contemporaries in terms used by Edith Sitwell in describing the nineteenth-century eccentric John Mytton: "racing, driving, jumping, hunting, chased always by a high mad black wind." Hunter, horseman, fisherman, naturalist, T. H. White was a connoisseur of arcane skills who saw nothing odd in training his hawks by methods which, as his biographer tells us, "Shakespeare would have found traditional."

These stories—the first such gathering—all but one ("Nostradamus") appearing in America for the first time; three of them heretofore unpublished anywhere—reveal White to have been fascinated by the past, entranced by the English countryside and enamored of rural pursuits, and charmed by the world of children. Almost all of these stories are mixtures of these concerns; characteristically, most are infused with White's predilection for the grotesque or supernatural; characteristically, too, all of them are imbued with a unique enthusiasm.

Judging that historians tend to dehumanize the humanities, White regarded himself as an antiquary and not an historian. But although some of his stories set in the historical past contain misstatements of fact—some stemming from a misapprehension of the significance of certain events—a severe

7

taking-to-task of White fails to take into account that by acting as antiquary he relieves himself of the need to observe strict historical accuracy, and is free to charge his pageant of the past with actual historical figures. Indeed, it is a jaded reader whose curiosity is not whetted sufficiently to send him scurrying to the sources to learn more of the people to whom he has been introduced by White. How very many readers, now middle-aged, must have made their way to Malory by way of *The Once and Future King*!

White's obsession with the past is demonstrated in "The Maharajah," which, although its action takes place in the 1930s, seems very much a picture of the India of White's own Raj childhood (born in Bombay in 1906, White was the son of a district supervisor of police, the grandson of an Indian judge); in "The Spaniel Earl," with its background savagery and grace of seventeenth-century England and its portrait of the "sauntering" Charles II; in the springtime lyric "Nostradamus," set in the sixteenth-century Provence of the Pleiades; in the frankly Gothic "No Gratuities," the scene of which is Fonthill, William Beckford's eighteenth-century pleasure dome; in "Not Until Tomorrow," with its setting of fourteenth-century England at the time of Wat Tyler and John Ball; in "The Philistine Cursed David by his Gods" and "A Link with Petulengro," both taking place in the nineteenth-century England of eccentric and gypsy; in "The Black Rabbit" and "The Point of Thirty Miles," both of which are set in the early years of the twentieth century.

Especially with "The Spaniel Earl," "The Troll," "The Black Rabbit," and "The Point of Thirty Miles," White makes the reader extraordinarily aware of nature—nature not always idyllic, but frequently "red in tooth and claw." These stories were written while White was teaching at Stowe (1932-1935); it was here that White first plunged into what would become a lifelong passion, the study of nature. At Stowe, too, White, supported in this endeavor by the income from the books he wrote, indulged himself in the pursuits of a toff—hunting, fishing, shooting, flying. It is easy to see in these stories the incorporation of his experiences.

The charm which children exercised on White's imagination is clearly discernible in the fact that in at least eight of these stories children are employed either as main characters or in strong supporting roles. In three of the stories—"The Spaniel Earl," "Not Until Tomorrow," and "A Link with Petulengro"—the children portrayed are the offspring of nobility or royalty. "The Man," another story whose main character is a child, is more obviously autobiographical, and reflects the childhood of White himself: after receiving a judicial separation from her husband in 1923, Constance White took her small savings and, together with a distant cousin, began working a pig and poultry farm.

To establish a reality acceptable to the reader is sufficient challenge for most writers; deliberately to warp and tilt that reality, and yet maintain the reader's suspension of disbelief, is beyond the talents of all but a very few. Of those writers who in our century have succeeded in tilting commonplace reality and making us observe it from new and disquieting perspectives, those whose names most quickly spring to mind are: Algernon Blackwood, M. R. James, Saki (H. H. Munro), Lord Dunsany, John Collier, and Roald Dahl. Drawn irresistibly to the portrayal of the misunderstood, the ridiculed, the

9

frustrated, White followed in the tradition of these writers and, on the basis of stories like "Soft Voices at Passenham," deserves to be numbered among their company.

But to my mind, it is the enthusiasm which White brings to his stories that is the single most important reason for his continued popularity as a story-teller: his enthusiasm is genuine, it is intense, and it is contagious. White's is the joy of a lonely host welcoming a benighted traveler. We are given lodging; we are warmed beside the fire; by candlelight we are conducted up the creaking stairs; we are shown our room; we are bade goodnight. There is no reason not to sleep, and soundly. But we stay awake—or dream. We are guests under White's spell. One is put in mind of Francis Bacon's comment that "there is no excellent beauty that hath not some strangeness in the proportion." There is much excellent beauty in these stories.

Austin, Texas
March 1980

Kurth Sprague

The Maharajah

The Maharajah seldom bought one of anything. Even Rolls Royces he generally took by the half-dozen.

He was a small, charming, roly-poly man, with bilious, toffee-colored eyes like a spaniel's, and plump, brown, silky fingers—the skin delicate and softly wrinkled—on which the fabulous rings were tightly countersunk. When he sweated, he sweated all over, through his baby skin, with a delicate, inoffensive dew. His clothes fitted him superbly. They always looked brand new: the jodhpurs spotless, the brown boots shining as if from the shop window—polished by what patient, leisurely, devoted labor—and the immaculate silk shirts changed three times a day. He had twenty-four pigskin dressing cases, full of cut-glass bottles with gold stoppers. He used Rowland's Macassar Oil on his hair and scented his handkerchiefs with eau-de-cologne. He moved neatly, neatly flicked open his gold lighter for the cigarettes of his guests without ever failing to catch a flame; was a natural rider, polo-player and cricketer: Harrow and Cambridge. He was not one of the greater rajahs, who were said to own swimming-baths full of diamonds and pearls, but he did have enough jewels to fill an ordinary bath to the taps. He was good at winter sports, chemin-de-fer and tiger-shooting off elephants. He had a slight cast in one eye, and there was a blue mark on the

11

bridge of his pug nose, like a gunpowder mark. He was about fifty. When he took off his turban, it could be seen that his hair was coarse, like horsehair.

The Maharanee, his second wife, was a girl of twenty-seven, once a typist, who had been born of middle-class parents in Seattle. She had married him for the grandeur of the thing, for the wealth, and because she believed that India was like the Arabian Nights. She was anemic, untidy, a feminist more or less stunned by now to the life of the harem, but unable not to nag about it, and she was going to have a baby. She was terrified.

They hated each other with mortal hatred.

Now that the romantic aspect of the marriage was over, she loathed and dreaded him for sexual reasons, for his color, for smelling faintly of cardamom seeds, for not "respecting" her, for being her master, and for what she considered to be oriental vices. Her soul writhed when the brown hands touched her.

He, on his part, his virility hurt and scorned, hated her for humiliating him.

He could have bought her up, and her whole family into the bargain, seventy times over. His power in comparison with hers was infinite. But he was brown. Even the bathful of gems and Harrow and Cambridge, even his ancient lineage against her parvenu background, could not compensate for the antipathy of their skins.

She had not tried to humiliate him in the first place. She had simply done so. The spontaneous shudder of her look was more murderous to his manhood than any calculated insult.

In comparison with himself, she was of no social importance or breeding or culture. But for several hundred years the white skins had ruled and looked down upon the colored ones, making a world-climate of superiority. His soul, like hers, writhed at the inescapable, unfair, global premise. She really did consider herself superior to him—an unforgivable situation between male and female in the East—and, worst of all, her body shriveled up his body, by dreading it.

Dr. Arbuthnot was summoned from Bombay in 1938, to attend the confinement of the Maharanee.

After the day and nightlong, sweating miles in the grimy railway carriage, and the tepid water with grit in it, and broken fans, and screens like a meat-safe; after the flies and the stinks; after the endless desert journey from the railhead, in the sixth Rolls Royce, which had gold taps for attar-of-roses long parboiled and encrusted, after the blazing sun and squalor and color and saffron smell of the bazaar, he was wafted to the gates of the palace—where mounted sentries in barbaric splendor, their dyed beards in ladies' hair-nets, saluted with curved swords.

The palace had been built in 1873. Its builder—one of those rajahs celebrated by Kipling, tutored by an Englishman, liberalized by John Stuart Mill, loyal to the Queen-Empress—had employed a Victorian architect of the first class—an expert on gothic waterworks and lunatic asylums built in red brick. Unfortunately, the architect had been old. He had recently married a young wife, and his Indian summer had been a proliferous one. On the waterworks, on the asylum, on the gothic buttresses, on the bricks which were blue as well as red, varied by encaustic tiles, his eroticized imagi-

13

nation had grafted the Brighton Pavilion, the Caves of Ali Baba and several stately Pleasure Domes after the manner of Haroun al Raschid—to celebrate his nuptials, and also his emancipation from the architectural solemnity inspired by the style of the Law Courts. He had died exhausted shortly afterward. His brain-child—not unlike a French railway terminus in some respects—stood in a park which hoped to look as if it had been landscaped by Capability Brown. But it was a landscape in peepuls and neems, banyans and plantains and frangipani, whose fauna were not the deer and domestic cattle of England, but chained cheetahs, and fighting elephants in vast stables, and cobras instead of rabbits in the parched grass. Where Brown might have planned a Palladian temple for the vista, there was a blackened patch on the hillside where goats were slaughtered.

Dr. Arbuthnot was not a brilliant physician. He was the kind who knocks about in the colonies, or is a captain in the R.A.M.C., or a coroner, or a police surgeon, or anything else in government service. But he was friendly, popular, well-meaning and equal to his lot. Some people said afterward that the Maharajah had chosen him because he was stupid. But he was shrewd if not brilliant, and he had the pawky tenacity of the lowland Scot. He attended his surgery hours regularly, defended his spare time outside these hours as best he could, and drank his pegs at the Byculla Club with even-minded good-fellowship.

The Maharajah did him the honor of meeting him in the echoing hall—which had cast-iron pillars in the shape of palm trees, and large numbers of stuffed tigers, realistically grouped.

"My dear fellow, how kind of you to come! And in this

heat too! I do hope you have had a good journey? That dreadful railway! How is the Presidency? How is dear old Malabar Hill?"

The doctor, who was accustomed to anxious and effusive husbands, said only: "How do you do, Your Highness."

"You must let them show you to your room at once. You will want to 'wash your hands,' eh? An exhausting trip. You must 'repair its ravages,' doctor, before we 'trespass on your good nature.' "

"Your Highness is vairy kind."

"I have put you on the east terrace. A little pavilion there, my dear chap, in the Scottish baronial style, after your own heart. Only two rooms, I am afraid, but entirely by yourself. 'East, West, Home is Best.' We want you to be quite at home, master of your little domain. Just a sitting-room and a bed-room, and of course your own kitchen. You must ask the servants for anything you need."

The marble terraces fell in tiers to a square tank, in the middle of which stood a statue of Lord Curzon. The lawns, watered twice a day by bhisties, frail skeletons in clean linen, were miraculously green. On the roof or pot-lid of the Scot-tish pavilion, a peahen moved her head jerkily from north to south. As usual, the taps in the bedroom did not work.

Dr. Arbuthnot said to the Khitmagar, "Pani lao"—and set-tled in.

The ground floor of the palace was neither European nor Asiatic. Every kind of *bijouterie* or *objet* or knick-knack jostled against every other kind and every other size. Tiger skins and Louis XVI chairs and snuff-boxes and model railway trains;

Rembrandts and Landseers and prints from *La Vie Parisienne*; brass idols and Buddhas; crystal chandeliers and pink gas-brackets; gorgeous thrones supported on elephants and silver épergnes in the shape of the Taj Mahal or Euston Station; perfectly empty rooms for some reason forgotten, and rooms absolutely packed with unopened crates from Fortnum and Mason's or Rowland Ward's; gleaming gunrooms with a hundred weapons of every kind, and marble ballrooms with filigree arches and inlaid mother-of-pearl; a palm-court with copper spittoons; traces of every period since Victoria, from every part of the world: masks from Tibet, musical cigar-boxes from Paris, ivory models of the Crystal Palace, round leather shields with four brass bosses and bull's hair on them, assegais, boomerangs, suits of armor, kudu horns, collections of cigarette cards, croquet mallets, kukris; exquisite brocades and native embroideries and saris and gold lamé and Balmoral tartans; alabaster statues of Psyche and custom-built refrigerators studded with gems; oars from Cambridge colleges, with the names of the rowers painted on the blades in gold paint; polo sticks, cavalry lances, golf umbrellas, hundreds of binoculars and machines for making ice-cream or soda-water or hand-rolled cigarettes; an entire stuffed rhinoceros; speaking tubes which whistled, and telephones and enormous radio sets and a tape recorder; a library in which the leather-bound books were false, but opened to reveal a sumptuous cocktail bar; Aubusson carpets and Persian rugs and Axminster, all covered with linen sheets; tapestry punkahs and electric fans and an air-conditioning plant which did not work; deep, leather chairs in the smoking-room, like a London club, baroque chairs, fragile ballroom chairs in gold leaf, carved chairs of teak, horsehair sofas, sociables, rocking-

16

chairs, ivory stools, a commode originally made for George IV, and bamboo chairs with long arms to support the occupant's feet and holes for his chota peg: everything was clean, tended, dusted, protected against the plagues of insects, and, if mechanical, mostly out of order.

On the upper floors, the Orient descended like a cloud of scent.

There, through a green baize door, typically silent, the deep carpets and artificial lighting of blind corridors whispered of secrecy. There, it was the women's house, the purdah, the place of keys and fingers to the lips. Doors opened and closed, footsteps were noiseless, hidden eyes watched, ears hearkened.

In her bedroom furnished by Heal's, the Maharanee lay with her face to the wall.

"My dear, this is Dr. Arbuthnot, whom I have told you about. A real doctor from the Presidency! A white man, through and through."

She moved her head negatively on the pillow, not looking around. The ayah, sewing by the bedside, stood up without a word and went.

"Dr. Arbuthnot will soon 'put paid,' no doubt, to all distressing symptoms."

Her limp hand, palm upward on the coverlet, moved pettishly.

"We must repose our faith in the doctor, my dear, in the wonders of European science."

Arbuthnot watched his plump face, wondering whether he saw there, deep in the black, oblique eyes, some hint of love or rage, hatred or contempt or supplication. But when the eyes met his, there was only politeness. The Maharajah shrugged, deprecating and courtly. "Women," he seemed to say. "You know what it is."

He withdrew in silence. Even if he was rotund, he was a ruler. He held in his state great powers. The dove-gray suit from Savile Row did not entirely hide a dignity, even a grandeur, foreign to Savile Row. It came naturally to address him as Your Highness.

The Maharanee proved to be a difficult patient. She let herself be examined without cooperation, heavy as a log, refusing to speak. Except for her condition, which was advanced, she was thin and collapsed. The pigmentation of her skin was suitable to pregnancy, but there seemed to be a peripheral neuritis. He wondered whether she drank. Hysteria? These memsahibs, he thought, who hitch themselves to coffee-colored potentates and then discover that they are in a different world, and hate it! How frightfully difficult it must be to submerge one's unconscious mind in an unrelated, incomprehensible, alien, even hostile subconscious—a subcontinent of other minds—to emigrate one's soul, as it were, into the unsibling soul of India. No wonder if they sometimes took to the bottle.

He stood looking on her with a Scottish sentimentality, pulling his lower lip. Poor woman! It was bad enough to live in India, exiled from the bannocks of the Lothians, even with the company of British clubs. But to live without a white face anywhere, absolutely surrounded by absolute strangers, out of touch with their customs and affections and institutions and modes of thought! One might as well put a goldfish into sea water.

Her replies were shakes of the head, or nods.

18

She only spoke once, fretfully.

"They are listening."

Nobody could have been kinder, more affable, than the Maharajah. He seemed to take to Arbuthnot, and lay himself out to win him. A fresh bottle of Haig's whisky was on the bedside table in the pavilion every evening, and every evening an invitation to dinner came, printed on pink paper speckled with gold—the royal coat-of-arms with its howdahed elephants as supporters embossed at the top. The motto was: By Strength and Sagacity.

"You were at Edinburgh, doctor? I am a Cambridge man myself. Wonderful days, wonderful university! The happiest days of my life, I always say. No doubt you will have played cricket?"

"Maharajah, we mainly used to drink beer."

"Beer, of course! The wine of the British Isles. Perhaps you would prefer it to the champagne you are taking? Of course you would prefer it: how thoughtless of me! We have some excellent lager, always on ice."

In a minute, without a sign from His Highness, the butler was pouring it out.

"And what do you make of my little wifie?"

"Her Highness is out of sorts, of course. Highly strung women are affected in different ways by pregnancy. We must build up her strength."

"The constant vomiting, doctor; is 'morning sickness' usual in the later stages?"

"In some cases, it does persist."

19

"You would consider her symptoms hysterical, perhaps?"

Dr. Arbuthnot cleared his throat.

"The Maharanee," pursued his host, "is a woman of strong character. We love each other dearly. Perhaps imaginative? Perhaps a little out of her element in this ferocious land of ours? We must all 'rally round' to combat her nervous state; but it is you, Arbuthnot, on whom we shall rely to 'pull her through.' "

A silver railway train, running on methylated spirits, was used to carry the port wine around the table after dinner. The doctor watched it doubtfully, crumbling his bread. He was anxious to be impressive. He wanted to pull the doctor-trick with a proper bedside manner, to put up a good show, and do the best for his patient. But he was an honest man and a cautious one.

"We are a devoted couple," said the Maharajah firmly. "It was a 'love match' from the start. Beautiful Seattle! They called that mountain Olympus in those days, but I understand it has been renamed. I should be desolate, quite *bouleversé*, if anything happened to the Maharanee."

He twirled the stem of his wine glass with flashing fingers.

"But imaginative. She is jolly imaginative, Dr. Arbuthnot."

In the evenings, sipping his whisky alone on the terrace and watching the flying foxes gliding from the mango trees, the doctor found himself pondering about his patient. He tried to imagine her life as a girl, among drugstores and ballgames and "dates" and the Daughters of the American Revolution, or was it the Ku Klux Klan? How different all that antiseptic world of toothpastes and sterilized milk and vegetables packaged in cellophane, and, yes, of blunt, superficial judgments, from the putridity and savagery and subtlety of India! What a vast step from the neighborhood societies and the ladies' bridge clubs to the feminine intrigues of purdah, and the almond eyes secretly calculating, illiterate, profound. And was it *possible* for goldfish to live in the sea? How could that toothpaste mind endure the blood-red chasms of betel-nut when her attendants opened their mouths? How could she, year after month after week, endure, persist, even survive, among foods, scents, temperatures, humidities, sounds, thoughts, movements, silences, clinking bangles, bare feet, bodily habits, spiritual attitudes, filth, flies, dangers, lusts, cruelties, loyalties, kindnesses, insights and conventions, all inimical, uncousinly, allergic to her own? Ah, the poor wee lass, he thought, sighing much among the fireflies, with half the whisky bottle gone, dreaming of Peebles and Hogmanay and Burns.

At state banquets, when twenty or thirty sat to dinner and the Maharajah stood to receive them under the chandeliers, wearing his famous emerald with its aigrette on a white satin turban, Arbuthnot was seated half way down the table. But they often dined tête-à-tête.

"In your profession, doctor, you become accustomed to death. It is a hazard of the trade, to which you have to harden yourself. In India we are accustomed to it also, and it comes so quickly. So many people die here, among our hundreds of millions. We swarm like flies, and die like them. Dead bodies in the Ganges, burning ghats, vultures on the Towers of Silence: we are conditioned to the knives of Shiva, the Destroyer.

"But I am a kindly man, doctor, by nature compassionate. All these stuffed animals in the palace here, and the guns and weapons, they belonged to my father. He was a 'chip off the old block.' For myself, I often think that I will give up shooting altogether, even tigers.

"Few tigers are really dangerous, poor things, It is only the sick and aged tiger, maddened by rotten teeth perhaps and too decrepit for his natural prey, who may become a 'man-eater.' Besides, it is their nature. We must all accept the facts of nature, don't you think?

"I am quite devoted to tigers, Dr. Arbuthnot."

One evening there was a pigskin dressing case in the pavilion. He opened it with curiosity. The hairbrushes and comb, the razors, soap-dish, camping mirror, bottles for hair-oil or astringent, were backed, bound or stoppered in gold plate. His initials were on every piece: J. R. A. He closed it regretfully.

It is a bribe of some sort, he thought: I must not accept expensive presents.

"Maharajah, you really should not send me sumptuous gifts like the dressing case. Your Highness must save up several lakhs of rupees to pay my bill, when it is presented. The bill will be surprising enough, without the additional kindness."

22

"My dear Arbuthnot, I have dozens of such cases. Besides, the brushes are already engraved. You must oblige me by accepting such a trifling 'token of our esteem.' Her Highness particularly wishes it."

"Her Highness . . ."

"Come, come, you will be seriously offending us, if you 'look this gift horse in the mouth.' "

The doctor was not a Scotsman for nothing; he said laboriously.

"I have made it a rule, sir, never to accept presents from patients. Such rules are essential in the profession of medicine. I feel sure Your Highness will understand, and excuse me."

The acute eyes clouded for a second, seeming to sum the situation up and confront it. The plump hand waved dismissively.

"As you please."

"A natural gratitude . . .' began the doctor awkwardly.

But the Maharajah was all smiles once again.

"It is we who must be grateful to you, Arbuthnot, to the honest North Briton. How seldom do the scruples of a native Indian compel him to refuse a gift! You will hardly believe the cupidity, nay, the venality, with which I am surrounded. It was only this morning that I discovered my Prime Minister, the Dewan, was actually making a profit on the palace stamps!"

"An eleemosynary . . ."

"Honesty," stated the Maharajah, "that is what we are lacking in Mother India, since the great days of the Raj. I do not conceal from you, Arbuthnot, that we princes are far from anxious to rid ourselves of British rule. A great pity it

23

would be, a betrayal one might almost say. We still remember in the palace here the days of my grandfather, when your esteemed Resident, Mr. Wilson, was, as it were, 'a father to our country.' There was a man for you, Arbuthnot, a 'heart of oak.' Diligent, incorruptible, selfless, devoted to the welfare of the state. And Lord Curzon, there was another man: we have a statue of him in one of the tanks. So imperial, so dignified! Can you imagine Lord Curzon pinching stamps?

"No, no. 'Perish the thought!' I am an honest man myself, transparently honest, and I can feel instinctively for that great Viceroy. Besides, the viceregal letters are never stamped. They come O.H.M.S."

In the pavilion after dinner, the dressing case was gone. Instead, in a morocco case ornamented with the princely arms, there was a solitaire diamond ring worth several dressing cases.

The doctor sent it back without comment.

Next day, there was an invitation to dinner.

He was turning over symptoms, as honest doctors do. He was not a brilliant diagnostician. Chronic gastroenteritis with hyperemesis gravidarum? Dyspnea and cyanotic flushing with edema of the face? Could dysentery be complicating the pregnancy?

The Maharanee sighed and silently wept, the tears running from the outer corners of her eyes. She held his hand in her thin, pigmented one. She pressed it.

As she pressed, the swollen eyes slid sideways, suddenly

24

vivid, quick, intelligent, packed with meaning. They slanted on, and swept back from, the window curtain.

He stepped to the window and drew the curtain.

The ayah, motionless behind it, pressed the palms of her hands together, as knights-in-armor hold them on cathedral tombs, and bowed with lowered lashes. The caste mark on her forehead had trickled down her nose, which had a ring in it. She left the room without a sound.

"I understand," said the Maharajah, "that my wife is objecting to her attendants? So necessary, however, don't you think, my dear chap, for a woman in Her Highness's state of nerves?"

He had got over the sulks and had commanded a review or gymkhana, apparently to impress the doctor.

After the heat of the afternoon, with its dust devils funneling across the plain and the still lizards transfixed on baking stones, only their throats throbbing, the prince's brigade passed the reviewing stand, where the Maharajah, in a horse-tail helmet with a spike and wearing the sash of his own order, stood at attention, three paces in front of his guests. The English brigadier in battle dress, a mercenary soldier; the mechanized company, neat and splendidly disciplined, their gun barrels lowered in salute; the infantry in their new-fashioned berets with the insignia of the state; the lancers, more barbarous, jingling, pennons fluttering, bits frothing, manes tossing: the private army swung before them with a professional steadiness which would not have disgraced the household troops. The climax before sunset was a charge of the cavalry, who, from the opposite end of the polo ground, thundered directly down upon the saluting base in a drumfire of battering hoofs, their harness glinting in a haze of dust, their teeth and eyeballs flashing in savagery: until, at the last moment, when death seemed certain for the spectators, the squadrons wheeled to left and right, cloven by the saluting Maharajah.

He was sleek and pleased with himself.

Tilting a sundown tankard of brandy and champagne, he fixed what seemed to be a meaning eye upon the doctor.

"You see, Arbuthnot, we princes even now are not entirely tied down. We still have traces of—what shall I call it—power?"

"Your Highness has a splendid body of men."

"I have always been interested in power. Perhaps it is because I was 'born to the purple.' My ancestors, of course, had absolute power: the power of life and death. All that has been altered in modern times, unfortunately, to a large extent. Would you believe it? The death sentences in my own state can be appealed to Delhi.

"Death, on the other hand, in India, is often sudden and unexplained. Our coroner's inquests, Arbuthnot, are hardly up to European standards.

"Do you notice," continued the prince, "that the pundits are always quoting Lord Somebody-or-other's aphorism about power? 'All power corrupts, but absolute power corrupts absolutely.' They seem to get some satisfaction by applying this to Hitler."

"It was Lord Acton."

"Indeed. And do you believe the aphorism, doctor?"

26

"We-ell . . ."

"I cannot credit it for a moment. After all, the human race has power over animals. You are an Englishman, my dear fellow, or rather a Scotsman, and no doubt you have some spaniel or other dog at your beautiful home in Bombay. You have absolute power over the creature. But has this corrupted you? Do you torture it? Do you starve it? Do you capriciously take its life? No, no, my good friend: I am sure you are perfectly charming to your dog, and that, far from being corrupted by it, you are ennobled.

"History itself teaches us the stupidity of Lord Acton's sweeping statement. Was the Emperor Augustus corrupted? Was Louis XIV, *le roi soleil*? Yet their power was absolute: no man might 'say them Nay.' "

"Now that you mention it, Maharajah, I suppose the Dictator of Portugal . . ."

"Exactly. A 'jolly good fellow.' "

He held up the silver tankard, humid outside from the iced champagne, and examined it thoughtfully, his head on one side.

"I am a good fellow, Dr. Arbuthnot," he said, "but I have my modicum of power. It would never cross my mind to take advantage of it, of course. Yet power, after all, is something, is it not?"

After dinner, there was a torchlight tattoo.

The guests, who were British officials, native politicians and representatives of American companies, sat wreathed in their garlands of marigold and jasmine, heavy with scent. The smell of woodsmoke from bonfires and pitch from torches mingled with the piercing sweetness of the flowers. The pods of the lebbek trees, invisible around the polo ground, rattled in the night breeze. Hurricane lanterns lit the perimeter, like an air-strip for night flying. Within the rectangle of twinkling dots, a mounted squadron performed their musical ride with torches, while the royal band, garish with plumes and epaulettes, rendered an individual version of the "Lily of Laguna." Clash, clash went the cymbals; jingle, jingle the harness; and the noble horses, infiltrating, weaving and countermarching, tossed the proud arches of their necks. They were dressed in standing martingales.

Then there was the tent pegging.

The pegs, with lighted rags wrapped around them dipped in paraffin, flamed in the spicy darkness. The black-avised cavaliers, looking huge on their black steeds, came with a rattle and thunder out of the night, their lances leveled, their eyeballs scarlet, the saddles creaking and the stirrups clinking. For a moment they were silhouetted in fire and splendor, and hammering horseshoes battering their ellipses on the crumbling earth, and then they were past, with a flick of the wrist, with a knack, as the meteor peg swept up backhanded in its upward arc on the point of the spear. "Hai!" was the cry of triumph as the darkness swallowed them again, the lance proudly erect with its flame above their heads, while a rustle of polite hand-claps pattered around the spectators.

"Neat," said the Maharajah. "I am fond of everything that is neatly done."

In the sick-room next morning, Dr. Arbuthnot examined the curtains and the cupboards. Then he sat beside the bed.

"Maharanee . . ."

"Please don't call me that. If you knew how I loathe it!"
He was at a loss.

"My name is Joyce. Joyce Neuberger, really."

She rolled her head on the pillow, the tears pouring out to
soak it, and all at once she was talking through her sobs.

"Nobody has called me Joyce for seven years. Nobody
loves me. Nobody to trust. Maharanee this, Your Highness
that. They hate me. They are hateful, hateful people. I would
like to kill them all. He calls me Flame of the Forest! But he
hates me too, and I hate him. The dirty nigger! I could tell
you . . . You wouldn't believe . . . they don't respect
you, doctor, not the natives don't. They don't understand the
American Way of Life."

He patted her hand.

"I done the best I could, doctor. I guess I was too young to
be married, when I was. But I done my best."

"I am sure the Maharajah is devoted to you."

She turned her head to look at him in amazement.

"Come again?"

"His Highness talks about you with great affection."

She had lifted her head to look at him in real surprise. Now
she dropped it back on the damp linen and turned to the wall,
relapsing into silence. Her pulse and the thermometer and the
stethoscope were rituals which she accepted with indifference, her eyes fixed on a spot on the wallpaper, out of
focus.

He sat beside the bed as silent as herself, tapping his teeth
with the ear-piece of the stethoscope.

"Joyce," he said eventually, "you will have to pull yourself
together, or you will be ill. Nobody hates you. You must put

29

these fancies out of your mind. I know it is deeficult to live among strangers, but you must think of the baby. You do not want to harm your own baby, do you, who will be the next Maharajah? Do you? Joyce?"

She would not answer.

His Highness seemed to be in confiding humor after dinner, inclined to play with his toys. They worked the silver railway train together, sending the port wine around and around the table in an aroma of methylated spirits, until the cloth caught fire. They put it out with port.

They walked through the suites of the *piano nobile* with the Dewan and the Brigadier and the British Resident, while the Maharajah demonstrated his mechanical contrivances and lectured on the progress of science. "Ave Maria," sung by Dame Nellie Melba, was played on a phonograph with a tin horn shaped like a convolvulus, after which a radiogram of enormous size, custom-built with tigers' paws for feet, told them the news in Hindustani. They lighted gas-brackets still in working order, and switched on the flood-lighting of the garden fountains—which were turned off. Cigar-boxes played minuets for them, telephone bells tinkled in remote stables so that His Highness could make unnecessary inquiries about linseed mash, a Victrola played Mendelssohn's "Spring Song," an astonishing contrivance in a large glass case full of kettledrums and trumpets gave a mechanical rendering of *1812*, a letter was dictated to the tape machine for transcription in the morning, a confusing telegram was transmitted by buzzer to the distant railway station—waking up the operator, who took it down wrong.

30

The Maharajah

"The wonders of science," said the Maharajah. "What changes we have seen in our own lifetime, what progress in the 'march of mind'! Remind me to order a larger airplane, Dewan. Would you like to have an air wing, Brigadier, to expand the army, or do you suppose that this will be unacceptable to our honest friends in Delhi?"

After the other guests had been dismissed, His Highness insisted on a nightcap with his physician. They sat in the smoking-room, surrounded by polo sticks and the photographs or pedigrees of horses, while the seltzer water poured its legions of bubbles up the amber glasses.

"Such a lot of entertainment! How rightly does the greatest of poets sing, 'Uneasy lies the head that wears a crown.' You will pity me, doctor, when I tell you that in all the twenty-four hours I can seldom count on fifteen minutes to myself. Family life? Devoted as I am to my family, devoted as all we Hindus are to the family ideal and to the sanctity of womanhood, to the procreation of life as a sacred necessity, I have little time for the softer pleasures on which my heart is really set. The moonlight in Seattle! The warm pulsation of a female breast! I often wonder whether I have acted rightly by my beloved wife, longing to cast aside the cares of state and to take her once again through Europe on a protracted 'honeymoon.'

"But we were talking of Science, Arbuthnot, of the Progress we have noticed in the Twentieth Century. I must really show you a contrast. In my dear old father's day, we used to communicate with our servants by means of this."

He went to a mouthpiece on the wall, took out the stopper which was chained to it, and blew. The brown cheeks filled with wind, like the cherub's in an ancient map, the cross eyes

31

bulged, dust issued from the orifice, and, in response to some inaudible wail of a whistle, a voice from other quarters instantly quacked. He told it not to bother.

"But this," said the Maharajah, pressing a switch beside a round-mouthed speaker on the writing desk, "is our own latest 'gadget.' "

From the loudspeaker came the hushing hum of power, a cavernous and muted roar, on which there floated crackles and the steady, magnified surge of human breath. It paused and sighed.

"You are listening to the Maharanee. The palace, you see, is 'wired for sound.' I am keeping it as a little surprise for her, doctor, when she recovers."

She was propped on neat pillows when he came to her, and began to speak before he could say a word. Her blonde hair, dark at the roots since it was last dyed, was freshly combed. She was heavily made up.

"There is nobody behind the curtains. No, don't interrupt. I got to tell someone about it, before I'm done for."

"Maharanee . . ."

"You were talking about the baby yesterday. You said the soor-ke-bacha loved me. Well, you got to know how it is, doctor: I'd like to have you understand."

He tried to make movements of silence to her, gestures of being overheard, but she was not to be stopped. She was off in a cataract of fear and misery and hatred, irresistibly talkative. She wanted to say it quickly.

"It's a dancing girl, doctor. She's twelve years old. Such a ninny. And she's sly too, and sulky, with kohl and stuff on her eyes. I'm sure I don't know what he sees in her, not that I care. Put on so badly, too. I never would wear those jewels in my nose, and bare feet and bangles and everything, and painting your palms red. You have to keep your self-respect. But it's this girl, with her ways and her double-jointed fingers. She clicks them. He's not a gentleman, doctor. He makes me speak to her, and have her in the palace. Nautch girls, they call them, I guess. We called them something else in the States."

"Joyce . . ."

"No. You came here to meddle with me, and you got to understand. I don't blame the girl, really. Of course she wants to be married, God help her, though she little knows what she's taking on. Unless they like it. She's black like him, of course, so perhaps they have the same habits. I don't know about that Marie Stopes, but really! And the things they smell of!"

He was looking around the room in despair, wondering whether he could spot the microphone and hang something over it.

"To be the Maharanee for herself, that's what she's after. He wants it as much as she does, the dirty beast. But it's one wife only for the Hindoos, doctor, as you know, and I'm the one who stands between them."

His professional soul was exasperated as well as scared.

"You really must not burden me with confidences. It's a private matter. After all, I am here as a physician, not as a marriage-guidance clinic. I am here to attend your confinement. Your relations with the Maharajah . . . It is the pheesical aspect which I am fee'd to attend."

She said with calm astonishment: "But don't you understand? The sickness and everything? Obviously, I am being poisoned."

It was not possible to tell at dinner-time whether the Maharajah had been listening or not. He was in affable humor, and, avoiding the topics of his own good nature, power, and devotion to duty, held forth at some length on the new subject of helicopters, which he claimed to be the aircraft of the future.

"You must pronounce it hel-icopter, not heel-icopter, Dr. Arbuthnot. The Americans, as usual, are wrong. 'Heel' would be *helios*, Greek for the sun. The true derivation is totally different, but it escapes me. Another glass of port?"

Afterward, on the terrace outside the pavilion, the doctor examined his medical conscience. Women with grievances were natural liars, and pregnant women were prone to fancies. At one time or another, almost everybody in India came to suspect that they were being poisoned. It was a poisonous continent. His low-church, level-headed mind recoiled from dramatic interpretations—too canny to trifle with wild-cat theories, anxious to avoid unpleasantness.

The hyenas, circling the settlements of man, called in the early evening with their rising notes: Caw-ra, Caw-ra, Caw-ra.

Arbuthnot shook himself and went to bed, pouring a tumbler of whisky, almost neat.

His own vomiting woke him, in filth and agony. His stomach was on fire and his tight throat parching with thirst. There was blood in the vomit. The bowels were out of control, the pulse weak and rapid, the calves of his legs wrung with cramp. He noted these symptoms between spasms, and his dour mind, battered as it was by the tempest of the body, searched for an explanation. Doctors in the East think instantly of tropical diseases. Cholera, typhoid, dysentery? Well, with cholera you were certainly loose at both ends.

He drank from the neck of the whisky bottle, which made him vomit worse.

He sat on the edge of the bed with cold feet dangling, breathing quickly, his clammy head on frigid hands, forcing himself to think.

To think.

Arsenic.

He dragged himself to the bedside chair on which his clothes were laid, groping in the coat pocket for the small, black Burroughs Wellcome Diary which he carried. He leafed through it with numb fingers, his eyes betraying him, thin pages sticking together under the trembling thumb. Page 70. "Inorganic poisons—(continued). Arsenic and its Preparations. Symptoms: As for antimony." He cursed antimony. The cruelty of having to turn back to 69, discriminating with carrot fingers between the thickness of pages, filled him with rage. Crumpled at last to the right heading, which flickered before his eyes, he perused with infinite difficulty the symptoms for arsenic and antimony.

Antimony—the anti-monk poison: he remembered this scrap of information with unnecessary amusement, laughing deliriously, until he spewed again. He doubled over his belly.

But he had to think.

35

Was arsenic soluble in whisky? Would it tell him in the Wellcome Diary? He thought not. He whiffled through the closely printed pages, distinguishing very little. He shook the whisky bottle, which did seem to have a sediment. He threw it out of the window.

Treatment.

With agonizing persistence he found his way back to the seventieth page. But the small print baffled him, and the long words grew more and more meaningless to a collapsing mind. Gastric lavage and Ferric hydrate and Dimercaprol (B.A.L.), 2–3 mgm./kg. body weight by intramuscular injection as a 5 or 10 per cent solution in . . . What had all this to do with him? He had come equipped as a midwife. The book fell from his hand, as the calf-cramp arched him like a gaffed salmon.

To think.

Well, lie down and keep warm. Don't drink anything that has been put out for drinking, not even the water. Have some soda bicarb: there is some in the bag: and yes, there is a bottle of olive oil. An old campaigner, he had the habit of taking with him, when he traveled, olive oil and Worcester sauce. He drank it, gave himself morphia, lay down in the foulness of the bed, and resigned himself to the mercies of his maker.

It was a silent night—as silent as it ever is in India. The silence was a sound really, the thin, maddening noise of crickets. Against this background of pizzicato, a bull-frog in one of the tanks, evidently the chorus leader, said in a deep and measured tone: death, death, death. The sycophantic chorus answered him instantly in the treble: yes-yes-yes-yes-yes-yes. It was the brekekekek-coax, coax, coax of Aristophanes, except that the coax came first. The multitude paused to con-

36

sider this statement, while the crickets sawed. Then they came again, shrill answer to hoarse and heavy announcement. Death, death, death. Yes-yes-yes-yes-yes-yes.

The sun bounded over the rim of earth with a clang. The monkeys scampered over the trees. The peacocks screamed against the chatter of the parakeets and the wooing of the doves. The seven-sister birds, thrush-sized and dingy, hustled along the ground in twos and threes, paying no attention to anybody. Dr. Arbuthnot, exhausted and colored like a mushroom, but living, tottered out to the terrace, to greet the return of day.

On the terrace—and this was unprecedented—the Maharajah was taking a morning stroll. His blue cigar smoke hung fragrantly in the still air. His long shadow stretched across the lawns, mingling with the longer one of Lord Curzon.

"Good morning, Arbuthnot. Good morning, my dear fellow. 'The top of the morning to you,' as they say in Caledonia, or is it in Ireland? You have slept well? A beautiful day we are going to have: you can tell by the peacocks. The sunrise, the fresh air, the birth of Nature! By Jove, it makes one glad to be alive!"

Damn you, you slimy bastard, he thought weakly, with the querulous fury of someone who has been tormented—so you were poisoning her after all. You needed an ordinary G.P., not a specialist, so that you could kill her under my nose and have a proper European death certificate for the Resident. And then, when she blew the gaff, you had to silence me as well. Hers must have been chronic arsenical poisoning, mine was acute. You wily Oriental gentleman!

But as he grew stronger, the doubts returned. There were so many bugs in India. Could he have been bitten by something in the night, a hemotonic venom? There were always the tropical diseases. His brain churned wearily over the various possibilities—dysentery, a malignant tertian malaria? Besides, was it possible, in the present year of grace, that a well-known Rajah with an English education could try to do away with a popular physician from Bombay?

Possible or not, he decided, with an obstinate set to his jaw, I am from Peebles. I have given my oath of Aesculapius. Doctors from the medical school of Edinburgh do not lose their patients for nothing. That woman is under my care, and cared for she is going to be. The baby shall be delivered, and the Maharanee shall live, or Jamie Robert Arbuthnot will know the reason why.

"Maharajah, I am afraid that Her Highness is suffering from fancies. You know how it is with women in her condition. To put it bluntly, she thinks that she is being poisoned."

"You shock me, Dr. Arbuthnot!"

"It is veery unfortunate. But there it is. We shall have to humor her as best we can. I was thinking, perhaps, that if I took my meals in the Maharanee's room, sharing them with her, it would help her to take nourishment?"

"By all means, doctor: we must do whatever you say. Poison! How dreadful! You don't by any chance suspect the servants?"

"No, no. There is no question of suspicion. It is a matter of prenatal hysteria."

"Such an idea! Really, I am overwhelmed."

"Her Highness will regain the tenor of her mind when she has been delivered."

"So cheerful hitherto, so contented in our own little palace home! What can have put such thoughts into her golden head? Goldilocks, that was what I used to call her, Arbuthnot, in the happy days of our courtship. And now this horrible cloud between us. You do not think that she actually suspects myself?"

"Her Highness is in an excited state."

"So she does suspect me! Arbuthnot, Arbuthnot, how am I to face this sorrow? I must dismiss it from my mind: I must not hold it against her: I must remember that it is a delusion of pregnancy."

"That will be the very thing."

"My world," said the Maharajah, "is 'crashing about my ears.' "

"Then the arrangement will be," said the doctor, "for me to eat with the Maharanee in future. I shall miss our interesting conversations at dinner. Indeed, I think I had better cook for her myself, as a matter of reassurance. Fortunately I have several tins of Allenbury's food in my luggage, unopened, and perhaps you will be kind enough to see that we are supplied with eggs, *in the shell*. Even the question of liquids is suspect to her, poor lady, in her present derangement, so your excellent lager will come in handy. It will be easy to convince her that a bottle of aerated beer, if it had been opened for the introduction of foreign matter, would have gone flat. So long as the lager is up, Your Highness, she will be certain that it has not been tampered with."

The Maharajah wrung his hands.

"My Goldilocks!" he exclaimed. "But come, I must 'be a man.' "

"In case of accidents," added the doctor as an afterthought, "I have written to my partner in Bombay, mentioning these unfounded suspicions."

The Maharanee accepted his ministrations without gratitude.

"Well," she said. "I suppose I had better have the baby. He might let it live."

"I must warn Your Highness that the Maharajah has wired this bedroom for sound. There is a microphone somewhere. He has been kind enough to tell me so."

"It makes no difference. The wogs have a grapevine anyway."

"You put me in an awkward position. Besides, if His Highness really is listening, surely it is unwise—unkind—to hurt his feelings more than necessary?"

"Unkind?"

"The Maharajah has always spoken with kindness about you, in front of me."

She leaned forward across the bed-tray, on which she was playing a Double Demon Patience.

"Do you seriously believe, Dr. Arbuthnot, that he means to let me live?"

"Of course I believe it."

"And so you are cooking eggs for me in the shell, and quenching my thirst with unopened lager?"

"It is . . . It is merely a precaution, Joyce. It is to humor your. . ."

"Do you reckon to stay with us forever?"

"Of course not. That is to say, after your delivery . . ."

"How do you like your eggs cooked?" she quoted bitterly. "Who is going to cook them after you have gone?"

The forceps delivery was fairly straightforward in spite of the trouble, but the Maharanee refused to see her baby. The Maharajah was overjoyed.

"A daughter!" he exclaimed. "The answer to my inmost prayers!"

He shook the doctor's hand in both of his, his blood-shot eyes brimming with tears.

"Never believe, Arbuthnot old boy, that the princes of India hope only for a son and heir. Gone are the days of suttee, forgotten the wicked old customs by which the female infant stood in danger of being exposed. No, no, all that has been altered in civilized states like ours. I shall call her Esmeralda, a charming name, don't you think? She shall be the very emerald of my pagri. My state pagri, Arbuthnot, or should I say turban? These terms are rather confusing. How like her beautiful mother she is! The very same eyes! And the hair, although admittedly black at the moment, will no doubt turn to that flaxen glory which adorns the maternal head. 'Gentlemen prefer blondes,' my good friend, ha! ha!, do they not?

"God bless you, Arbuthnot, for all you have done for us. A new leaf now, the old trust and confidence! How is Her Highness? Am I allowed a little visit of congratulations? She no longer feels the . . . suffers from . . . suspects? Those unworthy suspicions! No, I see I need not ask you. All is forgiven and forgotten. 'The rain is over and gone, the time of the singing of birds is come.' Who said this?"

"I believe it is in the Bible."

"The Bible! The holy book. Do you know, Arbuthnot, I feel holy myself today, positively holy. When you return to your own people in the dear old Presidency, you must tell them from your heart that there is no great difference between the Hindu and the Christian, you must tell them so from me. 'Sisters under the skin.' The same reverence for life, the same charity of feeling. 'The greatest of these is charity.' How the sun shines now for the indulgent father—not forgetting the happy mother, soon to nestle that little forehead against the teeming bosom, with all her sufferings o'er.

"Come, we must toast the newcomer in a Rajah's peg! The ayah will take her back to the nest. My little Emerald! Farewell for now. Brandy and champagne! Or shall we take it with a lump of sugar and a dusting of cayenne? Perhaps you would prefer Black Velvet?

"Whatever you choose, doctor. You are a monarch of this palace for today.

"You must remain with us for a long time, Arbuthnot. Positively I shall insist upon it. You must lead my little girl, my wifie, back to the sanity we once enjoyed. It will be a 'primrose path' for all of us. 'Cheerio!'

"Some more champagne? That's it. That's it. 'Let something, something, something and joy be unconfined!' "

The squint was in the left eye, Arbuthnot decided, as the tears of happiness splashed gaily in the sparkling wine.

* * *

42

At the railhead, after the long journey in the sixth Rolls Royce, he discovered the dressing case among his luggage after all. He opened it with curiosity. Inside was the solitaire diamond ring as well. He sent them back by the Rolls.

Some months later, taking a sundowner at the Bycullo Club, he heard that the Maharanee and her child were dead. People said it was cholera.

A Sharp Attack of Something or Other

The senior partner claimed to be descended, on the wrong side of the blanket, from Talleyrand. To his sorrow, he was getting old.

He took out his gold watch from Cartier's, hardly thicker than a half-crown, and noted that it was 9:40. He telephoned.

"Susan?"

"Oh, Francis!"

"Henry left?"

"You know he always catches the same train."

"I know. Well, honey?"

"Francis, I can't come. You musn't ring me up like this, honestly you musn't. It's quite a small exchange and you don't know what might get about. After all, I *am* a married woman: I am his wife: you know how he hates me going out with you."

"He needn't know."

"Of course he'll know. He's under my feet all the time. How won't he know? Honestly I can't come, Francis; I'd love to, but honestly. No wool."

"Wool?"

"Over eyes."

"Henry," he said grimly, "needs to be put away for a bit."

When the junior partner reached the office, he was in a condescending humor.

"There's a hat for you," he said, putting the black, immaculate object on the desk. "Bought it this morning from So-and-So's. Best hatter in town. You want to smarten yourself up, Francis, now that you're getting on. Buy yourself a new hat and get your feet pedicured, ha, ha! It's wonderful what a new hat can do for an old man, old man. In the spring a young man's fancy, and all that. Curly brim. Latest fashion. Size six and seven-eighths. No less than five smackers at So-and-So's. The lot!"

He pulled off the size label and threw it in the wastepaper basket.

"You overwhelm me, Henry."

"Nuts."

The younger man hung it on the office hatrack and went to the floor of the Stock Exchange, bareheaded.

Francis looked at it for a long time, disliking its bouncy assertiveness, its vulgarity, its meanness, its brim. For it was mean: meanly valued for having cost five guineas. It was a cad's hat.

He rang for the secretary, who came, flashing in rimless, octagonal spectacles, acidulous, efficient, devoted to the head of the firm.

"Mr. Foster has bought himself a new tile."

"So I see."

"It is in the latest mode."

"I hope it will be big enough for Mr. Foster's head."

His poker face, the heritage of Talleyrand, examined her with what seemed to be benevolence.

"Are we busy this morning, Miss Vine?"

"There's only Robinson and Peabody."

"I can deal with them."

"There are the letters to sign."

"Yes."

He put the long fingertips together.

"Miss Vine, would you mind taking a taxi to Messrs. So-and-So's in Bond Street and buying me a hat exactly like Mr. Foster's, size seven and a half? Take it with you, if you like, to be sure of the pattern."

"Very well, Mr. Marchand."

"It will be a little secret between us."

When it was time to go home, Henry took the superb headgear from its peg and put it on his head with a flourish. It sank to the bridge of his nose.

"Good heavens," he said, "look at this thing. Only bought it this morning, and it's out of shape already. By God, I'll kick up a shindy with those baskets in Bond Street. You'd think that an expensive hat from So-and-So's . . . They'll have to change it for me, that's all. Bloody profiteers!"

He was late next morning, arriving with a grievance and a new hat, this time a midnight blue.

"They tried to say it was part worn because I pulled the ticket off. But I tore them off a strip. I gave them something to think about. They said that it couldn't have fitted in the first place, but it did. You saw me in it. Dirty crooks. Anyway, they changed it for this one in the end. I think it's better, don't you? You see the blue effect? It goes black in electric light, so you can wear it for a **show**. But I bloody well told them it was the last time I'd go to So-and-So's. You want to be firm with these people, or they take advantage. Insist on service, that's my motto, if you want to get it. However, as a matter of fact, I do prefer this model. It's kind of jaunty, no? Thought of getting yourself a new lid yet, old man? Just the job for the middle-aged spread."

When he had gone about his business, Francis said to himself, with a faint exclamation mark between the eyebrows, "Wear it for a show!" He rang for Miss Vine.

"Electric blue this time," he said, "please. Like the new one. Size seven and a half."

"Very good, Mr. Marchand."

When the blue hat sank over his eyebrows that evening, Henry snatched it off with a start. He looked sidelong at his partner, to see whether he had noticed, and retreated to the washroom, where he put it on and off again several times in front of the mirror. He took it home with him furtively, carried under the arm.

Before business opened next day, Francis was sorry to notice that the young man seemed depressed.

"Are you feeling all right, Henry?"

"Why not?"

"I thought you looked different somehow. I don't know why."

"Different how?"

"It's probably nothing."

"Perhaps I am a little worried."

"I mean, for the last couple of days, you seem to change."

"Change?"

"Swell up or something. Puffy. But it may be my fancy."

Henry asked abruptly, "Did you deal with Robinson and Peabody?"

"Yes. There was no trouble."

After a bit, he inquired, "Can people's heads swell?"

Francis laughed.

"Not yours, anyway," he said teasingly. "Forget it, Henry. It was an idea that crossed my mind, an optical delusion or something."

"If people's heads did swell, it would be pretty serious?"

"Nonsense. You are getting ideas because of the famous hat."

Henry took himself to the market and Francis went to the rack. The band of the blue hat, size seven and a half, was heavily stuffed with brown paper. He took the original (6⅞) from the deep bottom drawer of his desk, transferred the brown paper to it, and hung it on the peg. Size 7½ went into the drawer instead.

That evening, Henry did not don his headgear in the office, but went to the washroom, where Francis was too tactful to follow him.

He came out, dazed and pale, with the hat balanced on top

49

of his curled hair like a dodgem car on the Witching Waves. He might have been an Eastern houri carrying a pitcher to the well. He went down the stairs carefully, looking straight in front of him, without a word.

"What is dropsy?" asked Henry in the morning, after he had hung up the hat, now minus its padding. "Can you have goiter on the top of your head?"

He looked pinched, as if he had a hangover due to some attempt to drown his sorrows.

"Of course not."

"I looked up snakebite in a Boy Scout's Diary which I have, and it said there are two kinds of venom. They are called hemotoxin and neurotoxin. Viper bite is hemotoxin and it makes you swell up immediately. You have to suck it, and wash your mouth out with permanganate of potash. But how can I suck the top of my head?"

"What on earth are you talking about?"

"Besides, I don't think I have been bitten by a snake."

"Henry, are you feverish?"

"Yes."

"I thought you looked a bit queer."

"Do mosquitoes have hemotoxin?"

"I'm sure I don't know. Look, Henry, you are evidently out of sorts. Why don't you take a day off, and go to bed?"

"I shall carry on," he said bravely, "to the end."

While he was carrying on, Francis exchanged the fitting size for size seven and a half.

He came out of the wash room blindfold, the hat over his ears, like a horse in a straw bonnet. He groped his way down the stairs in awful silence, clutching a packet of permanganate of potash.

In the morning, the senior partner consulted his Cartier watch and lifted the telephone.

"Susan?"

"Oh, Francis!"

"Henry left?"

"Well, as a matter of fact, no. Or rather, yes. He's gone to a nursing home."

"A nursing home! Good gracious, not ill, I hope?"

"He thinks he is. It's too extraordinary. He says his head keeps swelling and shrinking. Do you think it could?"

"I wouldn't put anything past Henry."

"So he can't come to the office."

"Poor Henry!"

"And he's gone a sort of purple-brownish color, like permanganate."

"No wool?"

"Honestly."

"My poor Susan, this must be very worrying for you. You ought to be taken out of yourself."

No answer.

"Honey?"

"Well, Francis, I *could* come. If it didn't seem too heartless about Henry?"

The Spaniel Earl

"It is a piece of family history," she said, "that has always been kept a secret. But now that the family is over I don't see why it shouldn't be told. It's about the second Earl, the one in the picture by Lely which hangs on the staircase; if it's still there. There used to be a rare volume about him in the library, privately published, but my husband decided to keep it under lock and key. He let me read it when we were married.

"I'm not a reading woman," continued the Countess modestly, "or not for fiction, but for some reason or other I got interested in that book. It was a little brown thing, quarto I believe it is called, and there were several different books bound up in the one. The first story was by a fellow called Nashe, and the second was about the Siege of Breda. I must have read the whole thing through five or six times. I don't know how it was. The only other thing I can ever remember reading was a story called *Ulysses* that was lent me by my son. It's a long book, you know, but I liked a lot of it quite a lot. I think it was about a pantomime. But I don't think it was as good as the *Siege of Breda*. I can remember whole bits of that, as if I had learnt it by heart.

" 'Viriliously,' " declaimed the Countess suddenly, " 'they stood, pouldering with Musket, Pike and hand Granad, whilst the Cannon swept away divers ranks of the Burgundians, flying in the ayre like Phrygien Eagles in a Randon. Through the excremental Smoke of their combustible Paines the Enemy sallied forth upon them, but were ever repulsed back to their owne repugnable limits, with Martiall Affronts, and loosing of lives. And Loe, the guns played they thick day and night, bellowing Bellona's Musicke, against that great and high earthern Bulwarke at Ginnekin Port, whilst the Muskets beat continually as thicke on their faces as the Winter-hayle, which whiten the ground. There went Colonel Balfoure's foure halfe Cannons against the Windemill; there it came down with a rattle, and bruised the bones of some Burgundians, till their guts groaned againe.'

"It was that sort of thing," said the Countess. "Stirring, you know. Of course it was a bit difficult to understand; but then, so was *Ulysses*. I read it, as I say, five or six times.

"The bit about the second Earl was the best. Do you remember him in the Lely picture, with his grubby, round, snub nose and dewy eyes? Well, as a matter of fact, he was mad. He thought he was a spaniel.

"He lived in the days of the Stuarts, when people were still pretty barbarous; and he lived at Woodmansterne, in the country. Of course, that was before the house had been rebuilt by the sixth Earl, who stole two million pounds from the nation. It was just a Tudor house with a few ornamental additions to the porch and so on. The Scamperdales have generally been happier in the country than in the town, and the second Earl was no exception. He was a fine, sturdy boy, with natural advantages and a gentle heart. They worshiped him in the hamlet, and he used to ride out like a miniature gentleman, in a plumed hat and Spanish leather boots. Hawking and hunting, you know. I can't remember what they used to hunt, but it wasn't foxes. He was fond of hounds, almost from the cradle.

"But although country people are ten times better than town people in every way, they are still terribly cruel at heart: especially toward animals. They are horrible to badgers, for instance, and frogs, and sometimes cats. In the old days they used to get rid of unsatisfactory hounds by hanging them, just like Christians.

"That was what sent the second Earl mad. He was an advanced child of six, already accustomed to be dressed as a gentleman and treated as a possible tyrant. He was sensitive, as you would expect from those big eyes, and affectionate, and naturally inclined to be a little odd. His father had been a very strange man indeed, copious and Elizabethan. The boy lavished a lot of his surplus love on living creatures, particularly on hounds. He had a pet owl. One day he ran into the great hall, because there was a pandemonium there. There was a noisy mixture of screaming, laughing and ferocity: rather like a pig-killing, only much worse, because the screams were more human. They went to his heart as if the creature really understood, really suffered in pitiful terror and was betrayed. The pig squeals without expression, like knives on china; but this was a meaning lamentation, of a conscious heart. They were hanging a greyhound bitch whose temper was supposed to be uncertain. She was struggling pitifully, her svelte face bent sideways in agony and contortion. Her belly, with the neat double row of dugs, looked naked and shameful; as bare as a new dead pig in a butcher's shop, but alive and capable of sex. The steward and scullions had red, lustful faces, through which they laughed with protruding eyes, like the bitch's. The tail curled upward between the legs and touched the belly. She kicked like a dog dreaming of rabbits, spasmodically, with both feet together. She ran with her forefeet, snatching at the rope. She had stopped screaming when the cord grew taut; and now, as the scullions stood aside, there were only guttural noises and her lolling eyes to greet the second Earl.

"The child ran out again without a demonstration, and the incident seemed to be closed. He did not lose his reason at a stroke. He had dreams, I suppose, asleep and awake. He did not speak or forget. It was only gradually noticed; when he began barking in the night or when he seemed inseparable from the kennels. At first they thought it was a game, that the child was playing at Let's-pretend. His father even entered into it, and patted him on the head, calling him a Good Dog.

"One day they found him inside the kennels. He was still incapable of dressing himself, especially with those stiff, pompous clothes, but he had managed to pull off one of his Spanish leather boots. He was lying in the kennel enclosure, very ragged and disheveled, in the sunlight. He had torn one boot to bits, and was gnawing a dry bone, his eyes scowling upward from under his eyebrows so that they showed a red rim. There was a great fuss trying to get him out. Finally they had to fetch his father.

" 'Come, boy,' said the first Earl. 'This is naught.'

"But the child only growled.

"The old rip, who had made his fortune out of James the First, began to lose his patience.

" 'A pox,' he said, 'on this fooling. I shame to see it. Away to your chamber.'

"The growls became fiercer, from right down in the chest.

" 'That a Scamperdale,' said the Earl uncertainly, holding out a strangely misgiving hand to touch him, 'should be such a natural!'

"The child wriggled its body.

"It was the last straw for the Earl. The growls somehow had been possible, but there was something in the incipient wagging of the tail that was not to be borne. He snatched a whip from a groom and set about his son with a kind of terrified savagery. He seemed subconsciously to have guessed the secret; and now, in a panic, he was trying to whip it out of himself, out of his issue. He was exorcising devils.

" 'Obedience!' he cried. 'Obedience!' between every stroke.

"The little body, held by the nape of the neck, tucked itself in behind, doubled its wrists like the forepaws of a dog. It whimpered, wriggled, finally began to snap and bite. There was a great oath from the Earl. He dropped the child suddenly, together with the whip, and stood back stupefied, nursing his wrist. There were the bruised incisions on it of sixteen even teeth.

" 'Boy!' said the Earl, with his eyes wide and his great virile back beginning to crumble; but the thing crawled forward on its belly, and licked his hand.

"After that there was nothing to be done. He was an only child, the apple of his father's eye as well as of the countryside, and he was indisputably mad. The attempts to cure him were pathetic and terrible. Renowned scientists, who lived in the tradition of Dr. Lopez and Francis Bacon, prescribed innumerable remedies. They ranged from relatively harmless herbs and distillations of gold and snake's fat to confinement and flagellation. They were none of them successful. After ten years of it, his father consented to the inevitable.

"They built the child a special kennel, and imported a pastry-cook who made artificial bones out of cooked meat and pastry. He showed a tendency to be intolerant of clothes, so they imported a tailor also, who made him a fur skin out of the pelt of a Russian bear for winter, and a doeskin, which turned out to be a great deal cooler, for his summer wear. By easy transitions they weaned him from the real kennels, where he was always getting bitten by the hounds, to the artificial ones, and thence by slow stages to the house itself, where he was treated as a house dog. He used to sleep on the bottom of his father's bed. It was pathetic to see the old man, whose wife had died some fourteen years before, sitting in the paneled room on a winter's evening, in front of the log fire. There he would sit, with his hand on the boy's head, staring into the bright heatless flames of elm. And his only son, with his chin resting on his father's knee, would stare up at him with liquid, mute, adoring eyes. Occasionally he would nuzzle with his chin, at the same time wriggling his hinder end and making a scratching movement with his paw. The old man, who had seen so much of vice and fortune and glorious hazard, would raise his hand and pat again, or scratch gently behind the ears; until his son rolled over to the floor, and lay there, on his pelted back, presenting his belly to the delicious claw.

"The boy, who was now sixteen, had lived on all-fours for

the last ten years. This had a curious effect upon his anatomy. His wrists were unnaturally strong and padded, his fingers weak. His toes, calves, hams and the small of his back were muscular, and he had a kind of biceps at the back of his neck. The inside of his forearms, chest and abdomen were shrunk.

"Of course the lunacy laws as we know them did not exist. If you were a great man you were a potentate, and you made your own laws. You could afford to be a *lusus naturae* or a lunatic, so long as you had birth. Nevertheless, his son's inheritance worried the Earl. There were always cousins, claimants, unscrupulous people. Even the steward and the upper servants were not above suspicion. When the first Earl was gone, there would only be a mad creature who thought he was a spaniel, an inarticulate and defenseless beast, to carry on the line. It was not so much that the Earl wanted the line to be carried on, though of course he wanted it, but that he was fond of the poor moron. Would the boy be safe, could he continue to depend upon his simple kennel and pastry bones and kind treatment, when the great house was in the hands of a steward who was a servant only in name? The aging Earl imagined the boy neglected, whipped, or even put away, with the present servant then the master.

"Charles the Second was on the throne, the first English king to be an individual. One had only to look at the pictures, to see the change that had come about since old Scamperdale was young. There was nothing of his stammering father's official reticences in the new monarch's composition. The second Charles was a personality. He idled about Whitehall, relating his adventures with some redundance to a crew of toy dogs and monkeys and mistresses. He moved through his palaces, walking very fast, in a sea of playthings, like a man running in a doll's house. He called it sauntering. When he was tired of playing with his retorts in the toy laboratory, he would tickle the spaniels or a mistress, feed the ducks or listen to the singing-boys. He would sing himself, or go to the play and make shrewd comments on the *scena*. Sometimes he would talk to Sir Christopher Wren, or to Mr. Evelyn. He was killing time.

"Or changing it, at least. In the old Earl's boyhood, that incredibly distant period when the sandy monarch had made his fortune, the King had been engaged on business of State, a figurehead for reverence. Charles the First had maintained the tradition. Now, in 1665, this dusky, foreign-faced fellow had instituted a different procedure. You had only to compare his portrait with his father's. The martyred sovereign had somehow always been conscious of his clothes, sitting bolt upright in them with a stuffed expression, as a king should. The official robes had been the official King, drawing attention away from any human face. The son had changed all that. He cultivated a sweet disorder; seemed, by lolling a crease into it, to establish a personal dominion over his royal raiment. He had invented personality.

"Unfortunately personality seemed to bring other qualities in its train. Kings, by ceasing to be figureheads only, had become human again: and humanity was fallible. The decapitated Majesty would have been blushing all day at the conversation of Old Rowley. The martyr's son, the King of England, was nicknamed after the palace goat! Even the old Duke of Buckingham, the vacuous Steenie who had exploited the odd affections of two successive monarchs, might have been surprised at the behavior of the new one. The new Duke, for

instance, had recently seduced Lady Shrewsbury, and killed
her husband in a duel, which the lady herself witnessed in the
costume of a page. She had held the Duke's horse, not her
husband's, and had gone to bed with the victor that evening,
with the victor dressed in a bloodstained shirt which he had
worn at the slaughter of her spouse. Morals had become individual. There was Lady Castlemaine, lying flat on her back in
her coach, being driven around the park, with her mouth
open, snoring! In the old days, from a peeress of Scamperdale's youth, it would have been unthinkable. Station in life
had been a real thing then, an institution that existed by itself.
Now it was a matter of personal choice. Lady Castlemaine
had gone to sleep, not because she wanted to shock an institution, but because she had decided that this course of action
was, for herself, and in the circumstances, reasonable. Perhaps
she had felt stuffy and tired at the same time. She had produced a piece of her own conduct. Everybody nowadays did
the same. They pleased themselves. Buckhurst, Sedley and
Ogle swayed at a window in the Cock Tavern, without a
stitch of clothing, and blind-drunk, shouting at the populace.
Even the King was under the imputation of being so far
regardless of institutionalism as to have married two people
at once.

"There was little hope that such a society would reverence
the Scamperdale line. Would they see to it that the mad boy
continued to inherit, simply because he was his father's son?
Custom, succession, primogeniture and rank seemed unlikely
to make an appeal to the free-and-easy Charles. There were
no *bien-séances*, no traditions. It was difficult to have a right
reverence for the nobility when half of them were of your
own creation: in both senses of that term. Was it Rochester

61

who had made the famous remark, when the King was addressed by a deputation as 'The Father of his People'? Lampoons on royalty itself, by its courtiers!

"Still, there was no other King, and there was no other solution. The aged Earl made his way to London, where his distinguished bearing, arrogant white beard, and antique clothing created a sensation and a fashion that lasted for a fortnight. He presented himself before the nervous, gypsy-faced bundle of appreciations, and knelt down with difficulty on a satin knee. The King was touched. There was a grandeur about the old man's magnificent mortality: the terrible grandeur of human insignificance vanquishing the gods by pride. The King consented; and then, of course, forgot.

"So the first Earl of Scamperdale died, at the then almost unbelievable age of eighty, and there remained a kennel at Woodmansterne, guarded over by an absent King. The King had forgotten about it, but the servants had not, and this was all that was necessary to the purposes of the dead man.

"The second Earl's was a peaceful reign. Everything in the uninhabited house was kept just so, against the possible contingency of the boy's recovery. The servants were happy and industrious, ruled over by a steward who need never have incurred his master's suspicion. The second Earl was a spaniel, and they treated him as such. For some time there had been an effort to call him Your Lordship, but he refused to answer to the name. They called him Dowsabel, inappropriately enough, since the name is really a feminine one; but dogs' names are often misleading. *Douce et belle*. It was a pretty name, and it seemed to suit the boy. There can seldom have been a better spaniel than the second Earl. The steward used to take him for walks in the fields, every afternoon, and

he once caught a rabbit. His early efforts in this direction had
been touching, because he ran with such difficulty on his
short forearms. But as the necessary muscles developed, and
the others decayed, he became more agile. He used to run
with his hind legs splayed apart, so that his knees should not
knock his elbows, and with his head on one side. He found
this easier than keeping his head tilted back, and it gave him a
fairly good field of vision on one quarter at least. He caught
the rabbit by intelligence rather than speed, for he cut it off
some distance from its burrow and had the sense to run for
the hole rather than for the rabbit. He was a very intelligent
dog. He could beg, die for King Charles, and play Trust for
lumps of sugar. He did, as a matter of fact, eventually submit
to being dressed up in order to be painted by Sir Peter Lely,
but this made him feel foolish. The only thing that he hated
was his monthly bath.

"The King remembered him, as capriciously as he had
once forgotten. He happened to be talking about breeding to
Dr. Bovill.

" 'Porco Dio!' exclaimed the King (he was a cosmopolitan
sort of creature). 'We have forgot the spaniel Earl.'

"On matters of policy it seemed practically impossible to
stir Charles into action of any sort. Nobody knew what he
would do next, or if he would ever do it. Would the Duke of
Monmouth be beheaded or forgiven? It was impossible to
say. But when it was a matter of his own pleasure or interest,
the King could act with an impulsive violence that left everybody gasping. It was like his sauntering, a rate of excursion
that varied between five and six miles an hour and left the
members of his entourage, at intervals of a few hundred
yards, fanning themselves with their hats. Within three days,

which was a remarkably short space of time considering the conveyances of that age and the distance from Woodman-sterne to London, the second Earl was waiting outside the King's laboratory, on a red leather lead with a blue ribbon around his neck.

"The whole thing was done with a good deal of decency, for though Charles had few or no worries about his own respectability, he did object to humiliating other people. If Rochester had been allowed to be there, or even the Duchess of Portsmouth, there might have been talk, laughter and scandal. Nobody was there but Dr. Bovill. It was the kind of delicate consideration, even for an Earl who thought he was a dog, that made Charles an attractive character.

"The King came out of his laboratory, attended by three of his own little spaniels, and talked with a very gracious accent to the steward who was leading the second Earl. He asked about his lordship's diet and manner of life, showing a lively interest in his hunting proclivities and in the rabbit which he had been able to kill. The second Earl was asked to die for King Charles, and did so gracefully. The King bent down and scratched his ear. Then, whilst the afflicted peer walked around on stiff legs sniffing the three toy spaniels, the steward was subjected to a regular interrogatory. Was the Earl easy to manage, and did he have to be corrected? Was he a good watch-dog? House-trained? What was his age? Dr. Bovill, meanwhile, examined the young gentleman anatomi-cally, and made a series of notes upon the displacement of his muscles.

"The King seemed much interested in Scamperdale's age, which was now twenty-one, and proceeded to ask a delicate question. No, his lordship had never fallen in love. Had any observations been made on this subject? Yes; the household at Woodmansterne was divided into two camps. On the one side a large majority maintained that a comely virgin would one day materialize, who, by striking his lordship with her feminine charms, would cure him eventually of his disorder. This majority urged a continuous introduction of virgins, in a kind of nubile parade, in order that one or another of them might catch his eye. The other small and detested faction declared that his lordship would only fall in love with a spaniel bitch, and that it would be best to yield to the forces of nature.

"Had either of these two alternatives been tried? Yes; the one exhaustively, the other clandestinely, but neither with any success.

"His Majesty then made a few observations upon the brilliancy of his lordship's eye, ordered that the boy should be returned to Woodmansterne, and retired into his laboratory to discuss the matter with Dr. Bovill.

"Charles, time-serving and dilettante procrastinator, was at heart a philosopher. He would only live once, and it behooved him to live as best he could. He was a man, and he knew it, with a man's life and transcience under the formal crown. What was the good of making a fuss about kings and diplomats and foreign policy, when all these things could be dealt with by those who were interested in doing so, and when there was so little time to solve the riddle of the universe? It was his Latin fatalism, his experienced philosophy (had he not hidden in an oak-tree on peril of his life?) that drove him from mistress to mistress, from experiment to experiment, on those striding legs. He was an honest scientist, seeking after truth. His only vice was too much opportunity.

"So, when the really rather interesting psychological freak of the second Earl was brought before him, Charles took to it with avidity. It was just the sort of phenomenon which appealed to the scientists of the seventeenth century. Sir Thomas Browne would have discussed it seriously and sensibly in his *Vulgar Errors*, and the King was as interested and tenacious. He was a man of worldly judgments, like most secret Catholics, and he instantly singled out the material points. To him the salient interest was that of sex. He had no desire to cure the Earl. For one thing, there were plenty of normal Earls, and only one who believed himself to be a spaniel. For another, the boy had remained a dog for fifteen years and a cure was improbable. The King, with his strange mixture of moody restlessness and humor, was delighted by the toy, diverted by it, and at the same time sympathetic. He was sorry for the Earl, who was evidently charming: with the sweet appeal and dependence of a good dog. It gave His Majesty a sense of responsibility.

"There was very little that one could do for a dog, except find it a mate. Apparently, neither human beings nor other dogs would do. It was Dr. Bovill who hit on the tentative solution. The Earl of Scamperdale believed himself to be a dog: the future Countess would have to believe herself to be a bitch.

"The investigation was set on foot with industry and expedition. A royal commission, presided over by Dr. Bovill, went through Bedlam with a fine-comb. There was a woman there with hydrophobia, but she had only just been admitted and died at once: this was the nearest that they got. A minority of the Commission thought that if the human-bitch were cried in all the towns and villages of England, something might be done. The majority decided against this, after consulting the King. Charles, with those attractive scruples of his, disliked the idea for the Earl's sake. It seemed somehow too common and public. After all, Scamperdale was an Earl: and on top of that there was the recollection of a fierce rheumatic knee, bending in white satin to a monkey face; an old intransigent knee that had bent to Charles the First in its maturity, and, earlier still, to ginger-headed James, in gallivanting silk. His Majesty kept the investigation royal. Agents were dispatched, traveling in a tedious and sober secrecy, to the courts of Europe.

"Slowly, in the course of two years, the possibilities began to materialize. In Naples there was said to be a woman who had given birth to a girl-child with the head of a mongrel. Alexis of Russia discovered a village in Siberia which was entirely populated by recognizably human beings who appeared to bark. A tribe was reported in the Far East, probably the Ainus of Japan, which was said to be covered with hair. Alfonso the Sixth received letters from Goa about a Brahmin who walked upon his elbows and knees. Francesco Cornaro wrote from Venice of a boy with a tail six inches long.

"It was from Scotland, in spite of all these worldwide researches, that the eventual solution came. There was on the slopes of Lochnager a crofter woman of forty winters who believed herself to have been possessed by a werewolf. The girl-child who had been the issue of this union was the wicked wonder of the district, as far as Morven Hill and Ben Macdhui. She had been stoned on three occasions, and once, in early childhood, left for dead. She spoke no human tongue, ran on all-fours, and was supposed to worry sheep. Only the unaccountable affection of maternity had kept her living in the bitter northern world. The tiny but-and-ben had been besieged by troopers from Braemar, and a minister of Dundee itself had denounced the witch-woman with the fruits of her wickedness from the Sabbath desk. The mother barricaded her door, protected the poor unnatural offspring in all the power of her aboriginal widowed womanhood. The dour religious crusaders, who had marched from Blair Atholl and Ballater against the inveterate enemy of man, laid faggots around the rough stones of her little house; lighted them with the fierce ribaldry of licensed beastliness; stood around with sticks and muskets to extirpate the ungodly couple in a sadistic orgy of religious fear. When the smoke was intolerable and the reddish stones the close walls of an oven, the mother opened her door. She stood there, snarling and disheveled, with her gray hair in wisps, the type and picture of the devil's dam. They shot her through the heart. The mad maid was crouching in a corner, and her they stripped. Naked, which she did not mind, repulsive, as she was by birth, grinning with a trebled lunacy, they took her to the lock-up at Braemar, to be burned in state.

"The King reprieved her, but not without a struggle. The Scottish glens were remote in those days and difficult to subdue. She was reprieved and bundled into a coach. The coach, staggering over the Devil's Elbow and through the Spital of Glenshee, carried its burden into Perth. She was guarded by a troop of horse. All the way through England the cavalry jingled by the side of the black box, and the box itself swayed on its inadequate springs, and the vulpine creature inside the box could be heard mumbling over its raw bones. If the door was opened, she hid herself in a corner and snarled: a dangerous, grating snarl, like the passage of two rough surfaces over one another. It was impossible and unsafe to coax her out. At Doncaster there was a new moon and she howled all night.

"The King went to Woodmansterne to conduct his experiment. He slept in a rose-velvet bedroom with a silver toilet-set and silver mirrors. In the morning the coach arrived.

"They took the second Earl into the great hall, which was on the ground floor directly within the porch, and they brought the black coach to the porch door. A file of troopers stood on either side of the coach, with sabers drawn, so that the only exit was the entrance to the hall. They evicted her with a rustic fork.

"The King and Dr. Bovill, with a few members of their suite and the steward and the upper servants, stood in the minstrels' gallery above the hall. A groom with a drawn sword and an ancient pistol was stationed at the still-room door, in case interference should be needed. There was an uproar outside, with shouts, commands and banging of sticks. The porch door, which had been open to the sunlight, swung quickly to. In the darkness, under the dim Tudor roof, there were two creatures living.

"She stood still, whilst her eyes accustomed themselves to the half-light. The second Earl, who had risen from his corner by the fireplace at the first noise, walked toward her with his head down: a stealthy and dangerous approach. She smelt him before she saw. Her eyeteeth, which were unusually long, bared themselves in a wolfish sneer. She drew back, bewildered by so many things that had happened to her so lately,

69

with her flank against the wall. Poor thing, she was not only a wolf, but a trapped one; not only a trapped wolf, but a Scottish wolf, in a foreign snare. The second Earl came up to her with a suspicious growl. She snarled, rigid, with averted head, glaring out of the corners of her eyes. The Earl halted within a yard. He sniffed and grumbled. She was as still as marble. He walked around her in a semicircle, on stiff legs, and sniffed her whilst she hunched her back. He stood aside also, for a moment, and looked at her out of the corners of his eyes. The two beasts remained motionless. Then the boy dissolved; walked up to her without a trace of fear; scratched her with the fingers of his paw. She flew at him at once. Her teeth, meeting in his shoulder, caused the King to make a hurried movement of anxiety. But the second Earl rolled over on his back. He wagged his bottom in a friendly gesture, smiled with a vacuous expression, and opposed no further efforts to the feminine vagaries of the second Countess of Scamperdale."

Success or Failure

The house they lived in was called Colenso. It was in a suburb of London near Wembley and was shaped like a wedge of cheese. The red, jerry-built roof sloped at a sharp angle which had been thought artistic in 1920. All the houses in the road had the same kind of roof. They were semi-detached. The road was called Laburnum Avenue. Each house had a rectangular strip of garden behind it, sixty feet by thirty feet, with wooden fences between them. They were cultivated in different ways. Some of the slatternly ones just had long grass and poles to hang out the washing, but many of them were proud of themselves, and tried to be better than their neighbors. The garden of Colenso began at the top, near the house, with a small strip of lawn carefully mowed. Then there was a neat patch of gooseberry and raspberry bushes, with three apple trees. Next there was a bed of potatoes and peas. At the bottom of the garden, there was a chicken house with eight hens in it and a little shed where Mr. Briant did his carpentry. In the summer, there was a fancy garden hammock or swing-seat on the lawn, and some croquet hoops.

Everything about Colenso was beautifully kept. The linoleum in the hall and on the stairs shone with a wax finish. The brass bowl in the sitting-room window, with a fern in it, was polished twice a week. Nobody sat in the sitting-room, unless there were visitors, and then some imitation Crown Derby china was brought out for tea, while the visitors perched on the hard, tight, clean, Drage chairs, which smelled of new cloth and furniture cream. The kitchen, where the family life was really lived, was as shiny as the sitting-room. The grate was black-leaded every day, and its brass bits gleamed with Brasso, as did all the knickknacks—like copper letter-racks in the shape of galleons, toasting forks with the Lincoln Imp on them, bits of metal off the harness of cart-horses, miniature candlesticks bought as souvenirs with the arms of seaside towns in enamel, and a bellows in beaten brass showing a lighthouse and some seagulls. The pots and pans and kettles were speckless. There was a special mat and scraper in the scullery, where Mr. Briant had to take his boots off when he came in from the garden.

Nearly all the houses in Laburnum Avenue had television aerials, which stood up like a forest of modern statuary called "Political Prisoners," or like the bare masts of futuristic tankers in a busy port.

Mrs. Briant was an ex-schoolteacher and had married her husband for the sake of being married. She was a house-proud Lancashire woman, who had a faint moustache and rather a wild, avid look, as if she might go mad at any moment. She was inclined to be the "life and soul" at Christmas parties. She jollied people along in a loud "funny" voice, crying "Ee" and "Bye"—a sort of imitation Gracie Fields, with the same kind of screech—and she ordered everybody to sit down or stand up or hide in cupboards or take a pencil and write down the names of twelve fish beginning with W. Under this veneer of camaraderie, she was as hard as nails. She allowed her husband to have a bottle of stout with his meals—it kept him out of the pubs—and she cooked for him superbly—but he had to sleep in a separate bed because of "hygiene," and she had taught him to believe that all males were beastly. They had no children.

Mr. Briant—she had married him rather late in life, when it turned out that there was nobody else available—was in one way a source of shame to her. He was a sewer man. For this very reason—he washed himself so thoroughly before he came home—he was cleaner than most other people in Laburnum Avenue, but she did not let him forget that she had married beneath her, and that she was a cultured person whose father had been a farmer, while her husband was low enough to work in drains.

They were far from being unhappy together. Most marriages are desperate affairs sometimes, when the glamor has worn off, but these two did have a clean, comfortable, warm home, with excellent food, and a loyalty to each other which was based on economics.

Mr. Briant was a stocky man going bald, with thick, foxy hair on his forearms, and he wore an apron when he was doing the washing up. He had his own hobbies, which he conducted in the shed at the bottom of the garden. He had a project or daydream about adapting the shed so that he could keep racing pigeons in it. Also he was a Freemason. On Saturdays he was allowed to go to the Freemasons or to the Bowls Club, where croquet was also played, and on weekday evenings they either listened to the radio together or else he did carpentry in the shed. He made stools and ornamental bookshelves neatly, or sometimes a special tour-de-force, like a cage for his sister-in-law's budgerigar. When they listened to the radio, he often wished that they could have the boxing commentaries, but Mrs. Briant preferred the readings from Dickens or one of the "diaries" which go on and on in England as serials—the "Diary of a Doctor's Wife" or "An Everyday Story of Country Folk." Mr. Briant was clever with his blunt fingers, which had golden hair on the back of the lower joints, but he was not clever with his head. He admired his wife for her brains. She was the leader in the marriage, and he accepted this, as he accepted her superior birth and education and her disinclination to have children. She preferred the radio to the TV.

One evening while they were listening to the radio, there was a talk on the Third Programme about Imaginary Children. It told about Charles Lamb, Kipling and Sir James Barrie, who had all three written about childless people, and how their characters consoled themselves by daydreaming of the babies who had never existed—about the might-have-beens.

It was Mrs. Briant who suggested they might invent a baby for themselves. The idea did not appeal to her husband at first, but he did not oppose it, and after a bit he caught on, with surprising imagination for such a humdrum man. Perhaps he needed a son more than he knew.

Their idea was to imagine a baby, and to let it live on, day by day, having the adventures which it would normally have had if it had been a real one, just like a baby on the radio serials. Both of them preferred a boy.

Mrs. Briant was a thorough woman, and she insisted on going through the whole procedure from the beginning. She only announced her pregnancy after three months, when she was quite sure, and she speculated about sex and names and provided herself with a layette—pink or blue—for the full time before she consented to present her husband with the expected heir. They talked it out every evening, in front of the kitchen fire, inventing incidents and testing them for probability, rejecting some, accepting others, until Mr. Briant was as excited as she was, by the time the nine months were over.

The delivery was a normal one, and the boy was born on the twenty-fifth of April. They christened him Arthur, after Mrs. Briant's father, and Pendlebury, after a distant cousin who had risen to be a general. He was a healthy specimen, weighing nearly eight pounds, and Mr. Briant was amazed by his mauve color, his wrinkles, his bedraggled hair and the perfection of his fingernails. When he remarked that the baby was mauve, Mrs. Briant was furious. She said that all babies were this color, which was not mauve, and for a whole evening there were strained relations in Laburnum Avenue.

They were model parents, devoted to the little life which they had conceived between them, and from the start they were determined to make it a successful one. Mr. Briant gave up having stout with his meals and actually put the money which would have been spent on it—real money—into a teapot on the mantelpiece, afterward investing it in savings certificates whenever the teapot was full. He did this in fact, not in imagination.

Mrs. Briant proved to be a good mother, though a bit fussy and dainty, as was natural in a schoolteacher. Mr. Briant often chided her for coddling the boy. She was a fanatical sterilizer and boiler of things. Also she insisted on a meticulous diet and regular habits, while her husband grumbled that his own large family at Southend, where he had been born, had been brought up more natural, and none lost.

As the child grew older and survived the countless hazards

and small troubles of infancy—the teething, the difficulties about food—he absolutely refused to eat vegetables or fat— and the day when he fell down in the toolshed and cut his forehead on a chisel which had carelessly been left about— Mr. Briant was full of remorse about this—they began to save up still more for him, again in real money, because Mrs. Briant insisted on a good education. In this she was not opposed by her husband. He knew the value of—he had before him, day by day, an example of—the power of education. Besides, he loved his son as much as she did. Nothing short of the best was to be good enough for Arthur.

The pool money, the stout money and all sorts of other luxuries were set aside, so that the boy could be sent to a preparatory school, as it is called in England, like a gentleman. Mrs. Briant had taught in a secondary school, which, instead of making her know better, had given her ideas about the other kind. She was an innocent creature in some ways. Mr. Briant, who could remember nothing about his own school except a girl called Mabel, accepted his wife's information on the subject. All the same, it was a struggle for them to pay the fees.

Luckily Arthur turned out to be clever. Probably he inherited it from his mother. He won a scholarship to Dulwich College.

He was clever, he was healthy in spite of the usual scares about mumps, chickenpox, etc., he was happy and—this was Mr. Briant's contribution—he was good at games. Mrs. Briant would not agree to his being the captain of the cricket team, but he played on it. All through the summer months, his father kept a record of his scores, grieving when he was out for nought and disputing the umpire's decision if he was given L.B.W. Mrs. Briant did not pay much attention to this, though she was pleased to hear of successes, in a general way.

They shared the usual disagreements of parents. Mrs. Briant was against corporal punishment on principle, while Briant was in favor of it—but he could not bring himself to do it, so there was no trouble about this. When Arthur was tiresome, as was perhaps natural in an only child, they talked it over quietly in the evening and made plans about how to cure him of it for the future.

One thing did lead to friction. Mrs. Briant did not want Arthur to be interested in girls or to do anything that was wrong. Mr. Briant absolutely refused to let him be a mollycoddle. He said that all boys were interested in girls—like Mabel. He said that any natural boy would tell lies sometimes and even pinch things, perhaps. They agreed on part of this eventually, as it gave them something to worry about. The girls were always a bone of contention.

Perhaps it was the girls who made the first rift in the lute.

As Arthur began to grow up and to be less dependent on his parents—less in need of his mother's protection—Mrs. Briant seemed to grow cooler toward him. It was not exactly that she was jealous of the girls. It was more as if she resented his being a male. She did not like it that he should have a life apart from hers. She lost interest in him as he ceased to belong to her protectorate, and even began to disapprove of him—perhaps to fear him, for being a man.

Mr. Briant seemed to love him all the more for being one.

It was at this point that husband and wife stopped imagining in harmony.

Being estranged from the masculine Arthur, Mrs. Briant

ceased to wish the best for him. The point was that she had it in her power not to give it to him.

She explained to her husband, while they were washing up in the tight, hard kitchen, that daydreaming was wrong when it became a wish-fulfillment. He did not know what she meant by this word, but he felt defensive and beleaguered, and held the wet cup with a damp clutch, in his blunt, russet fingers.

She said that they were just imagining Arthur to be clever and successful and good at things because they wanted him to be so. But few real people were like that. It was betraying the truth of their creation, she said, to make Arthur a superman who always went from strength to strength, just because they hoped for it. It was more likely that he would fail sometimes. He might fail often. He might be a failure.

As a failure, of course, she would have got him back into her protection. But she may not have desired this. She may have dreaded his successes, or envied them.

Briant was forced to agree that people did not usually turn out to be supermen. He was not one himself. From now on he fought a long losing battle on behalf of Arthur, who began to go from bad to worse.

He went to London University, again on a scholarship assisted by his parents, but he slacked there and did not do well. Mrs. Briant pointed out that children who were brilliant too early often used up their powers too soon. Also, she suspected that those unlucky girls might have got hold of him in earnest. He began to show signs of being a rotter.

As Arthur began to go to the dogs, his parents began to fall out about his doings. They reproached each other about his upbringing, quarreling about the might-have-beens. The quarrels were one-sided in a way, because Mrs. Briant provided the noise while her husband sulked, in silent obstinacy.

The boy did not get a good job. The best they could do for him was a clerkship in a bank. It was badly paid. The inevitable happened, and he stole some money to bet on the horses. Mrs. Briant had been afraid of this.

His broken-hearted parents were working in the oblong garden at Wembley when matters came to a head. There was the patch of neat grass, thirty feet by fifteen, which Mr. Briant was mowing. There was the crazy path with alyssum growing on it, the border of lupins, the clothesline, some potatoes and scarlet runners, and the small toolshed. The pigeon house had never been finished.

"Prison!" cried Mr. Briant. "Oh, Arthur! He must not go to prison!"

"God is not mocked," she said.

"What can he do—what can he do when he comes out?"

"We shall have to move."

"But Arthur never meant no harm."

"He will find no work as an ex-convict. We shall have to support him forever."

Mr. Briant said: "I will get him on the sewers. I can ask Mr. Brownlow."

"A sewer man," she said bitterly. "And then I suppose he will marry a schoolteacher—like you did."

Mr. Briant went to the toolshed for his croquet mallet. He bashed her brains out with it. It only needed one thump. He had to do this, in defense of Arthur. He could not afford to have two failures in the family.

79

Nostradamus

The soothsayer Nostradamus was dozing in his garden at Salon, about the time when Queen Elizabeth came to the throne of England. It was a charming garden, a charming summer evening, and a charming maiden of tender years went past the gate, demurely balancing her nice behind. She was going to the forest to collect firewood.

"*Bonjour, Monsieur de Nostredame.*"

"*Bonjour, fillette.*"

Silly old fool, she thought as she passed, giving an extra wag. Little girl, indeed! I am fourteen years of age. And not much does he know, even if he is supposed to have second sight, if he thinks that I am interested in the collection of firewood. The son of the Comte de Tende himself will be waiting for me at the charcoal-burner's hut—my own darling Claude—and I am, in capitals, at a Cross Roads of My Life.

She knew that Claude hoped he was going to seduce her there, and she may have had her own ideas on the subject.

She was a brown, firm, well-developed, miniature Venus, with a shiny black head smoothed tight, warm eyes, and a determined mouth—which had faint dark hairs above it. They were versatile lips, able to be shaped equally for sulking or for kissing, for tenderness or for obstinacy. Every curve was in proportion, though she was only five feet high. She was brave. She gave the impression of knowing what are called the answers. She did not know them very well. She was a honey.

At the charcoal-burner's hut, the son of the Governor of Provence was waiting in poetic ecstasy. These were the days of Ronsard and Clément Marot, so he was quoting verses to himself about Nymphs and Muses and the desolating passage of Time, which young people feel more poignantly than the old ones, who have less of it left. He was making up his mind to undo her with the following sentiment:

> *Le temps s'en va, le temps s'en va, ma dame,*
> *Las! le temps non, mais nous, nous en allons,*
> *Et tost serons estendus sous la lame:*

> *Et des amours desquelles nous parlons,*
> *Quand serons morts, n'en sera plus nouvelle:*
> *Pour ce, aymez-moy, ce pendant qu'estes belle.*

He was four years older than she was—a Quixotic, gentle youth, with shy eyes and a strongly developed sense of honor. He was even kind to animals, which was rare in the sixteenth century, and, left to himself, he could not have seduced a cockroach—far less raped it. What he really meant was that he hoped to make love to her very tenderly, if only she would let him.

Marie perceived these facts at a glance, when she was still several yards away from the hut, and they revolted her.

She said at once: "I am afraid I cannot stay long, because the dinner is on."

"But, Marie . . ."

"I don't wish to be pawed about."

"No," he said dubiously. He looked at the ground.

They sat on a faggot, side by side, and examined the woodland scene with constraint.

"I saw Monsieur de Nostredame."

"Oh."

After a time, he added: "Was he well?"

"He called me a little girl."

"And so you are a little girl, a darling little girl, the most lovely little girl in all the world!"

He tried to take her hand.

This made Marie angrier than ever. She had told him about the magician's insulting remark so that he would understand that she did not want to be treated like a child; and here he was doing that very thing. What a fool! She did not want a lot of quotations from Ronsard, she did not want to be treated tenderly, and she was not, was not, a little girl. However, she contained herself.

"Marie, why are you cross with me?"

"I am not cross."

"You know I would never do anything to hurt you—never do anything you did not want?"

She tossed her head. She knew it well.

"I promise."

Nincompoop!

"Marie," he said, desperately, "why are you like this? Please give me a kiss?"

She felt that things were getting better.

"Well, just one."

He got her hand at last, and hugged her gently, touching a

sigh of a kiss, hardly skin-deep, on the parted, moist lips. He felt hollow with love.

"Marie," he whispered:

> *"Marie, levez-vous, vous estes paresseuse,*
> *Ja la gaye alouette au ciel a fredonné,*
> *Et ja le rossignol doucement jargonné,*
> *Dessus l'espine assis, sa complainte amoureuse."*

Ronsard! She could have slapped him. She pushed him away, confining the kiss firmly to one, as stated.

"Marie!"

"Monsieur de Nostredame is a vigorous man for his age," she said. "He has had two wives and the first one had two children."

"Had she?"

It was no good. She gazed at a thunder-smitten oak without seeing it, her miniature foot tapping on the moss. Claude gazed at it too.

"What were their names?"

Oh, blessed God, she thought, give me patience. How do I know their bloody names and what does it matter anyway? Her hands picked in her lap. She looked down at them, paused, blushed, and surprised herself by relenting. Poor Claude! He was so soft, and in such a muddle.

"You may give me another kiss."

He lifted her strong, small, knuckle-dimpled hand to his lips and kissed it reverently.

"My little nymph," he said. "you do not have to let me kiss you if you do not like it. I only want to do what pleases you."

"But I do like it."

"Really?"

She nodded. She blinked her eyelashes.

He put his arms around her, at the neat waist, feeling the smock slide easily over what was underneath, which meant that there was nothing underneath except Marie. He began to tremble. His hand strayed uncertainly to nudge, to touch, the innocence of her breast. She curled herself to him a little, leaning back, looking into his eyes, blinking industriously.

He kissed her downward, properly, on the open mouth, his neck arching forward, hers backward, like a pair of swans.

"*Fillette!*"

She closed her mind to this. Evidently she was going to have to put up with it.

He wondered whether it was the right time to lift her skirt a little, perhaps an inch, above her knee? Others said that you had to stroke their bosoms for some time, before you went lower. He decided on the bosom, and began to fondle, rather like scratching behind a dog's ear to please it, and with the same intention. He did not know that this was boring her more than it bored him.

Marie put her arms around his neck, to lift her breasts, and stretched her legs like a cat, to lift her skirt. He absent-mindedly pulled it down again.

She realized that he was practically hopeless, and would have to be helped. She stood up in one wave of a movement, no clumsiness, and was sitting on his lap. Her arms, tight around his throat, made it difficult to breathe. He patted her bottom, her head over his shoulder, rather as one pats babies to make them break wind. He said in a strangled voice: "My little girl!"

"Do you love me, gentle Claude?"

He managed to say that he did.

She gave him more air.

After some time, he said: "Marie, this faggot is rather uncomfortable."

It was, in fact, printing a sharp pattern of twigs on him, and a knot or splinter had, he thought, with the additional weight, punctuated his left buttock.

They got up and lay down on the soft moss, side by side, face to face. He took his courage in both hands and lifted the skirt, without protest. Her dimpled knees, which she held together for the purpose of having them prised apart, filled him with rapture. He stroked, and his hand was beginning to learn.

Marie observed incautiously, to take her conscious mind off what was happening: "I do like poetry."

"Do you?"

She nodded and blinked.

And God, he was off again with the whole of Clément Marot's *Epistre au Roy, pour avoir est derobé* (130 lines)!

She leaped to her feet, she called him something dreadful, she told him to go away, she burst into tears. He stood in front of her aghast, spreading his hands, apologizing, asking what he had done wrong, promising that he had never really meant to seduce her at all. She forced him to go. She watched him, grieved, baffled and desperate, slinking off into the forest. She sat on the faggot and sobbed.

One of the village boys, who had been observing these maneuvers with interest from inside the charcoal-burner's hut, opened the door and came out. He took Marie by the wrist, twisted her arm, shoved her into the hut in front of him, and shut the door. Neither of them said a word.

Scarcely an hour after she had last seen him, Marie once more passed the house of Nostradamus, with a slight limp. She said demurely: "*Bonjour, Monsieur de Nostredame.*"

"*Bonjour, petite femme,*" replied the philosopher slyly.

No Gratuities

O my dear Sir, it was a most magnificent edifice! The tower was three hundred feet high! It fell down twice! The Gothick style, you know, similar to our ancient abbeys and other buildings of baronial importance. Such taste, such flair, such romantic imagination! Only there was an oversight about the foundations—they forgot to have any. It fell in 1801 and again in 1825, alas, for the last time. Many a visiting tourist has remarked to me, as you have done, that it was worthy of Vathek himself—in whose palace, as you remember, there was a lofty tower of fifteen hundred stairs, connected with it by a subterraneous passage! Thank you, I will join you in another glass. Not that the tourist has at all times been welcome at Fonthill—indeed, quite to the contrary. Allow me to propose the health of Mrs. . . . Er? No, you are not married? Neither was Mr. Beckford. Or rather, he was a widower of many years standing, and there had been the scandal, hem! Yes. But a very interesting gentleman, that I must say, interesting and *unconventional,* if we may put it so. Respectfully put it so. I always felt the greatest respect for Mr. Beckford. It was impossible not to feel it. That compact form, those flashing eyes, the limbs well-knit in classical proportions, though naturally somewhat stiffened by the effects of the advancing years, and his lips, my dear Sir—they were like *worms.*

Yes, the tourist has not at all times been welcome amid the howling winds, the stormy clouds and the profound darkness of our abbey—occasionally pierced by a glint of moonlight or by the faint glimmer of some taper! The gloomth, as Mr. Walpole used to call it. Not that Mr. Beckford and Mr. Walpole were on the best of terms—there was a coolness between them, being in the same line of business—I refer to their novels.

Tourists were discouraged, yes. Indeed, our invisible Caliph went to the trouble of erecting a wall around the property, which he used to call the Great Wall of China. It was seven miles in circuit, twelve feet high and crowned by a *cheval de frise*—a formidable obstacle.

You behold in me, Sir, an actual acquaintance of that famous recluse—if acquaintanceship it may be called. Yes, certainly it may be called that. Our commerce may have been unusual, but it was intimate, for the short period while it lasted, and I retain an image of that interesting man which time can never erase—until the grim reaper finally mows away all recollection, reducing every memory to the stubble of the Harvest Home.

He was a short gentleman, dressed in a green coat with brass buttons, leather breeches, and top-boots, and his hair was powdered.

Our encounter was not conventional, not in the sense in which that term is usually employed. I was a young fellow then, my dear Sir, and I had my share of bravado! The rumors of Fonthill Splendour, as we sometimes called it in Bath, the tales of its strange Abbot guarding his treasures like some oriental dragon against the public eye, of the princely objects of art there sealed away, and of the park itself—known by report to be a paradise whose lake was plentifully stocked with waterfowl and having a road thirty miles long meandering through its secret plains—all were impenetrable, but fascinating to us. There were spring guns scattered through the shrubberies and mantraps of the most ferocious description. They snapped legs off as neatly as Pinchbeck's patent snuffers snuff off candles. Mr. Beckford told me so himself.

I laid a wager of considerable sum, Mr. Er, that I would walk in those gardens, would even penetrate into the Abbey itself. I was a stranger to Mr. Beckford, Sir, at the time of laying it, but I made that wager. The effrontery of youth, perhaps, and *not* the conduct of a gentleman—as you may be thinking—but youth is full of curiosity. My nature has ever been an inquisitive one.

Many an anxious hour did I spend, Sir, watching the great gate in that prodigious wall, hoping that by some inadvertence it might be left unguarded. The spikes were sharpened and besides, my pantaloons! At last, one day, the happy moment came. The porter was ill, and his wife threw open the entrance to a tradesman, who, after depositing his goods at the lodge (no butcher or baker was allowed to go to the Abbey itself), retired, leaving the gate open, relying probably upon the woman's shutting it. Quick as thought I had passed the awful portals.

The park was magnificent, from the beauty of the trees and shrubs, and the manner of arranging them, along a ride five miles in length! I was met here and there by a flock of tame hares which Mr. Beckford used to feed—then pheasants, then partridges—and lastly came to a beautiful romantick lake, transparent as liquid chrysolite, covered with wildfowl.

I own I walked with circumspection.

No cry of hounds, no hoof of the foxhunter nor percussion of the sportsman shooting flying, was allowed to disturb the sanctuary. The privacy of those sacred surrounding uplands, planted with larch, spruce, fir and rarer trees from distant countries, was sufficiently preserved by the spring guns, and many a shrub did I examine attentively or pass at a distance, while my pace was regulated by a kind of *shuffle*, if I may describe it so, calculated to be a form of locomotion which would be the least likely to release a trap.

Bravado, yes, but then, I am not courageous. Would you call me a timid man, Mr. Er? Yes, I see you would—timid and talkative, perhaps, but not without my moments of rashness. Regrettable moments.

At length I made my way to the gardens, guided by the high tower of Beckford's Folly, and, not being able immediately to find the entrance, was leaning on a low wall that shut the gardens from the park, and taking my fill of delight at the gorgeous display—the gardens being in full beauty—when I was approached by a man with a gardening implement in his hand—perhaps the head gardener—who asked me how I came there, and what I wanted?

It was a shock! I had hoped to be undetected. There were numberless working men employed about the grounds, among whom I might have passed unknown. A trespasser, Sir, *inside* that frightful wall, which now imprisoned me as effectually as it had previously kept me out, and accosted by a person in authority who had penetrated my disguise!

"The fact is," I stammered, "I found the gate in the wall open, and having heard a great deal about this beautiful place, I thought I should like to see it."

"Ah!" said the gardener, "you would, would you? Well,

you can't see much from there. Do you think you could manage to jump over the wall? If you can, I will show you the gardens."

I looked over the wall, and found such a palpable obstacle—in the shape of a deep ditch—on the other side of it, that I wondered at the proposal.

"Oh, I forgot the ha-ha. Well, go to the door. You will find it about a couple of hundred yards to your right, and I will admit you."

Why did he invite me to jump into the ditch? I might have broken my neck.

I will spare you, my dear Sir, a description of those wondrous pleasure grounds through which the gardener now led me, the acres of hothouses, the Eastern blooms, the exotic fruits from other lands! Largely because I am no botanist myself. I gaped at all without comprehension, while the man named to me the various rarities, using their Latin and sometimes their oriental names. The spectacle was a magnificent one—but at the same time I was beginning to suffer from a sense of uneasiness. A small matter, Sir, but as a gentleman you will understand me. The sum total of coinage available in any of my pockets amounted to one florin. This amiable and evidently well-educated upper servant would certainly expect to be vailed—a gratuity I believe it is called nowadays, or even a "tip" by the vulgar—and I was increasingly doubtful about his probable reception of such a sum! Two shillings, Mr. Er, is hardly acceptable currency when dealing with a cicerone who talks Latin! I searched my pockets more than once, without attracting attention, but was only able to find a small memorandum book which I always carry—I considered presenting it to him as a memento, but somehow it seemed unsuitable. Besides, he had a memorandum book. He consulted it in my presence, while seeking the scientific name for a myrtle, brought there from Powderham, I recollect, so he told me, wherever that may be.

"Now," said my guide, "would you like to see the house? There are some rare things in it—fine pictures and so on. Do you know anything about pictures?"

"I think I do," I replied, mistakenly perhaps, "and I should, above all things, like to see those of which I have heard so much. But are you sure you will not get yourself into a scrape with Mr. Beckford? I have heard he is particular."

"Oh, no!" said the gardener. "I believe Mr. Beckford will not mind what I do. I have known him all my life, and he lets me do pretty well what I like."

"Then I shall be very much obliged."

I had won my wager!

But, oh my dear Mr. Er . . . Jones? Thank you. Oh, my dear Mr. Jones, how little that achievement seems to me today, compared with the wonders I was now to behold! You are a cultivated man, Mr. Smith, yes, I can see it in your eye, and it must stir your blood, aye, fire the most icy vein, to be told of that interior? The Octagon Chamber, originally intended as a chapel, a room soaring 128 feet upon a diameter of 30! The Western Yellow Withdrawing Room! St. Michael's Gallery! The Great Dining Hall, in which a vast fire perpetually burned, but it was much too cold to dine in—Mr. Beckford had to eat in the Oak Parlour, unfortunately the furthest apartment from the kitchen. The numberless rooms all fitted up so splendidly—one with minerals, including precious stones—another with the finest pictures—another with Italian bronzes, china, etc., etc.! At last we came to a Gallery that surpassed all the rest from the richness and variety of its ornaments. It seemed closed by a crimson drapery held by a bronze statue—but my guide stamped with his foot, exclaiming "Open!" and the statue flew back until the Gallery itself was seen beyond the drapery, extending 350 feet in length!

Now was the time when I began to regret my previous claim to be a connoisseur of pictures. My conductor pointed out to me the gems of the collection—the "St. Catherine" painted by Blunderbussiana of Venice, the "Doge" by Sucrewasser of Vienna, the "Gipsy" of Aldrovandus and the "Fifth Plague of Egypt" by Watersouchy of Amsterdam! I marveled in silence, I applauded the taste of the collector, and I wondered at the information of my guide, whose favorite among all those masterpieces was the well-known Raphael by Og of Basan.

"Why, bless my soul," said he, "it's five o'clock! Ain't you hungry? You must stop and have some dinner."

Yes, Mr. Brown, you have perceived it. It was none other. I was overwhelmed.

Mr. Beckford led me back through chamber after chamber, discoursing on their merits as we traversed them—on the innumerable doors of violet velvet covered with purple and gold embroidery—on the fine medals, gems, enameled miniatures, drawings old and modern, suits of armor, curios, prints and manuscripts—on the chimneys of the sitting-rooms, with their large gilt filigree baskets filled with perfumed coal—on the musick room and the chapel, where, on the altar, were heaped golden candlesticks, vases and chalices studded over with jewels. There were no mirrors. Mr. Beckford kindly explained to me that the wizard Athelrepo would only tolerate cabalistic mirrors, but he did not explain why.

What a story to relate to my circle at Bath! The charm and courtesy of my host were combined with a sort of awefulness of countenance which I find difficult to describe to you. His face was like a mask, Mr. Jones, a cupid's mask—the complexion smoothed, the eyebrows arched, the nose slightly protruding, and the lips so rosy! He spoke with the greatest distinction, in a low but thrilling voice, and his information upon every subject was extensive. How different from the ogre represented to us by the ignorant world, the terror of the tourist! Every word which fell from his lips was an unction which soothed you to belief. His treatment of the uninvited guest was the flower of consideration. The dinner was magnificent!

Wines of the rarest vintage, Mr. Er, delicacies served on massive plate—but rarer still was the conversation of the recluse, with its monks, nuns, ruined battlements, secret passages, horrid chasms, banditti, precipices, moldering graves, stalking phantoms, deserted wings, roofless aisles, bats, vampires, towering crags, tolling bells and artificial ruins crimsoned with gore! He spoke, among other matters, of "the fleshless jaws and empty sockets of a skeleton wrapped in a hermit's cowl." It was in some castle or other ending with O. He told me of evil banquets which he had attended, where the Venetian glass would crack as the poisoned wine hissed into it. He spoke of tales so horrid that he trembled while relating them, and had not a nerve in his frame but vibrated like an aspen! My head was in a whirl!

Of Mr. Beckford's actual reminiscences, I regret to say, I can remember little. The wines, the incense, the dimmish light by which he preferred to consume those costly viands, the music of a concealed oriental orchestra, and the appearance of a certain number of dwarfs and Italian noblemen—unless there may have been only one of each of these—contributed to confuse my attention, and I neglected at the time to note them down in my book of memoranda. I recollect that he told me he had been kind enough to invent and present the air of *Non Piu Andrai* to the composer Mozart, and that he had been taken by the architect Le Doux, in a closed carriage, by devious routes, to visit Cagliostro at the temple of the Illuminati. On another occasion he conquered the affections of a large lioness at the Jardins du Roi, entering her cage at any hour of the day to receive her caresses, which caused him in a fortnight to become the talk of Paris. He spoke much of the affections, and more than once he did me the honor to press my hand.

I was a young man, Mr. Smith, and fascinated by his condescension. It was believed that he had turned back the Prince Regent at Basingstoke, with a refusal to entertain him at Fonthill after he had already set out, yet he was spreading the treasures of his intellect before an anonymous trespasser. In this very palace had he received the immortal Nelson and his Lady Hamilton—on which occasion, the cortège was met by the band of the Fonthill Volunteers playing "Rule Britannia" and a *feu-de-joie* was let off, followed by "God Save the King." Here, in this very park, on that occasion, had the Volunteers lined the avenues, each with his flambeau, while the roll of drums echoed from the surrounding hills and Lady Hamilton performed her Attitudes.

Not that Mr. Beckford spoke very kindly of Lady Hamilton. He seemed to bear a grudge against the Sex, if one may put it so, except of course the nuns and other heroines who were generally pursued by vampires along the subterranean passages of the stories he related to me. A feeling man, Sir, even if his veneration for the Attitudes was rather critical, and he pressed me warmly to stay the night.

He pressed me, and I was honored by the invitation, but, as I explained to him . . . He did not listen to the explanation. Although by custom an abstemious man, he drained a final bumper of the scented wine, launching out into a rather confusing narrative about some people called Courtenay whose family motto was *Ubi Lapsus? Quid Feci?*—which he repeated to me both in English and in Latin. The worms of that Cupid's bow writhed as he repeated it. *What's wrong? What have I done?* He buried the powdered head in his small white hands.

I was explaining to him with emotion that our Philosophical Society at Bath, of which I have the honor to be Secretary . . . He did not listen. I was horrified, my dear Mr. Green, to observe that a torrent of tears was splashing into the jeweled chalice between his elbows.

The Louis Quatorze clock upon the mantelpiece struck eleven, the candles guttered. At last, Mr. Beckford drew himself together and, fixing me with a piercing eye, observed: "Not an animal comprehends me." He excused himself from the table and left the room.

I sat in the semidarkness of that vast dining chamber, Mr. Jones, while my shadow fluttered over the trophies on the walls. I pondered the unaccountable outburst, as I ponder it still, and at the same time reflected on the distance to Bath, turning over the florin that remained to me. I sat, and I waited, and the light grew denser, and the clock ticked. I drew my chair to the dying fire, to comfort myself until the return of my host. The time seemed endless and I may have dozed.

When I awoke, the room was in almost total gloom and a solemn footman, in powder and gold lace, was extinguishing the last candle.

"Where is Mr. Beckford?"

"Mr. Beckford has gone to bed," said the man, as he put it out.

The dining-room door was open, and there was a dim light in the hall.

"This is very strange," I said. "I expected Mr. Beckford back again. I wished to thank him for his hospitality."

But I rose, and followed him toward the hall.

"Mr. Beckford," said that functionary, as he threw wide the massy portals of the front door, "has ordered me to present his compliments to you, Sir, and I am to say that, as you found your way into Fonthill Abbey without assistance, you may find your way out again as best you can. And he hopes you will take care to avoid the bloodhounds, which are at loose in the gardens every night. I wish you Good Evening. No, thank you, Sir—Mr. Beckford never allows vails."

The Troll

"My father," said Mr. Marx, "used to say that an experience like the one I am about to relate was apt to shake one's interest in mundane matters. Naturally he did not expect to be believed, and he did not mind whether he was or not. He did not himself believe in the supernatural, but the thing happened, and he proposed to tell it as simply as possible. It was stupid of him to say that it shook his faith in mundane matters, for it was just as mundane as anything else. Indeed, the really frightening part about it was the horribly tangible atmosphere in which it took place. None of the outlines wavered in the least. The creature would have been less remarkable if it had been less natural. It seemed to overcome the usual laws without being immune to them.

"My father was a keen fisherman, and used to go to all sorts of places for his fish. On one occasion he made Abisko his Lapland base, a comfortable railway hotel, one hundred and fifty miles within the Arctic Circle. He traveled the prodigious length of Sweden (I believe it is as far from the south of Sweden to the north, as it is from the south of Sweden to the south of Italy) in the electric railway, and arrived tired out. He went to bed early, sleeping almost immediately, although it was bright daylight outside, as it is in those parts throughout the night at that time of the year. Not the least shaking part of his experience was that it should all have happened under the sun.

"He went to bed early, and slept, and dreamed. I may as well make it clear at once, as clear as the outlines of that creature in the northern sun, that his story did not turn out to be a dream in the last paragraph. The division between sleeping and waking was abrupt, although the feeling of both was the same. They were both in the same sphere of horrible absurdity, though in the former he was asleep and in the latter almost terribly awake. He tried to be asleep several times.

"My father always used to tell one of his dreams, because it somehow seemed of a piece with what was to follow. He believed that it was a consequence of the thing's presence in the next room. My father dreamed of blood.

"It was the vividness of the dreams that was impressive, their minute detail and horrible reality. The blood came through the keyhole of a locked door which communicated with the next room. I suppose the two rooms had originally been designed en suite. It ran down the door panel with a viscous ripple, like the artificial one created in the conduit of Trumpington Street. But it was heavy, and smelled. The slow welling of it sopped the carpet and reached the bed. It was warm and sticky. My father woke up with the impression that it was all over his hands. He was rubbing his first two fingers together, trying to rid them of the greasy adhesion where the fingers joined.

"My father knew what he had got to do. Let me make it clear that he was now perfectly wide awake, but he knew what he had got to do. He got out of bed, under this irresistible knowledge, and looked through the keyhole into the next room.

"I suppose the best way to tell the story is simply to narrate it, without an effort to carry belief. The thing did not require belief. It was not a feeling of horror in one's bones, or a misty outline, or anything that needed to be given actuality by an act of faith. It was as solid as a wardrobe. You don't have to believe in wardrobes. They are there, with corners.

"What my father saw through the keyhole in the next room was a Troll. It was eminently solid, about eight feet high, and dressed in brightly ornamented skins. It had a blue face, with yellow eyes, and on its head there was a woolly sort of nightcap with a red bobble on top. The features were Mongolian. Its body was long and sturdy, like the trunk of a tree. Its legs were short and thick, like the elephant's feet that used to be cut off for umbrella stands, and its arms were wasted: little rudimentary members like the forelegs of a kangaroo. Its head and neck were very thick and massive. On the whole, it looked like a grotesque doll.

"That was the horror of it. Imagine a perfectly normal golliwog (but without the association of a Christie minstrel) standing in the corner of a room, eight feet high. The creature was as ordinary as that, as tangible, as stuffed, and as ungainly at the joints: but it could move itself about.

"The Troll was eating a lady. Poor girl, she was tightly clutched to its breast by those rudimentary arms, with her head on a level with its mouth. She was dressed in a night-dress which had crumpled up under her armpits, so that she was a pitiful naked offering, like a classical picture of Andromeda. Mercifully, she appeared to have fainted.

"Just as my father applied his eye to the keyhole, the Troll opened its mouth and bit off her head. Then, holding the neck between the bright blue lips, he sucked the bare meat dry. She shriveled, like a squeezed orange, and her heels kicked. The creature had a look of thoughtful ecstasy. When the girl seemed to have lost succulence as an orange she was lifted into the air. She vanished in two bites. The Troll remained leaning against the wall, munching patiently and casting its eyes about it with a vague benevolence. Then it leaned forward from the low hips, like a jackknife folding in half, and opened its mouth to lick the blood up from the carpet. The mouth was incandescent inside, like a gas fire, and the blood evaporated before its tongue, like dust before a vacuum cleaner. It straightened itself, the arms dangling before it in patient uselessness, and fixed its eyes upon the keyhole.

"My father crawled back to bed, like a hunted fox after fifteen miles. At first it was because he was afraid that the creature had seen him through the hole, but afterward it was because of his reason. A man can attribute many nighttime appearances to the imagination, and can ultimately persuade himself that creatures of the dark did not exist. But this was an appearance in a sunlit room, with all the solidity of a wardrobe and unfortunately almost none of its possibility. He spent the first ten minutes making sure that he was awake, and the rest of the night trying to hope that he was asleep. It was either that, or else he was mad.

"It is not pleasant to doubt one's sanity. There are no satisfactory tests. One can pinch oneself to see if one is asleep, but there are no means of determining the other problem. He spent some time opening and shutting his eyes, but the room seemed normal and remained unaltered. He also soused his head in a basin of cold water, without result. Then he lay on his back, for hours, watching the mosquitoes on the ceiling.

"He was tired when he was called. A bright Scandinavian maid admitted the full sunlight for him and told him that it was a fine day. He spoke to her several times, and watched her carefully, but she seemed to have no doubts about his behavior. Evidently, then, he was not badly mad: and by now he had been thinking about the matter for so many hours that it had begun to get obscure. The outlines were blurring again, and he determined that the whole thing must have been a dream or a temporary delusion, something temporary, anyway, and finished with; so that there was no good in thinking about it longer. He got up, dressed himself fairly cheerfully, and went down to breakfast.

"These hotels used to be run extraordinarily well. There was a hostess always handy in a little office off the hall, who was delighted to answer any questions, spoke every conceivable language, and generally made it her business to make the guests feel at home. The particular hostess at Abisko was a lovely creature into the bargain. My father used to speak to her a good deal. He had an idea that when you had a bath in Sweden one of the maids was sent to wash you. As a matter of fact this sometimes used to be the case, but it was always an old maid and highly trusted. You had to keep yourself underwater and this was supposed to confer a cloak of invisibility. If you popped your knee out she was shocked. My father had a dim sort of hope that the hostess would be sent to bathe him one day: and I dare say he would have shocked her a good deal. However, this is beside the point. As he passed through the hall something prompted him to ask about the room next to his. Had anybody, he inquired, taken number 23?

" 'But, yes,' said the lady manager with a bright smile, 'twenty-three is taken by a doctor professor from Uppsala and his wife, such a charming couple!'

"My father wondered what the charming couple had been doing, whilst the Troll was eating the lady in the nightdress. However, he decided to think no more about it. He pulled himself together, and went in to breakfast. The professor was sitting in an opposite corner (the manageress had kindly pointed him out), looking mild and shortsighted, by himself. My father thought he would go out for a long climb on the mountains, since exercise was evidently what his constitution needed.

"He had a lovely day. Lake Torne blazed a deep blue below him, for all its thirty miles, and the melting snow made a lacework of filigree around the tops of the surrounding mountain basin. He got away from the stunted birch trees, and the mossy bogs with the reindeer in them, and the mosquitoes, too. He forded something that might have been a temporary tributary of the Abiskojokk, having to take off his trousers to do so and tucking his shirt up around his neck. He wanted to shout, bracing himself against the glorious tug of the snow water, with his legs crossing each other involuntarily as they passed, and the boulders turning under his feet. His body made a bow wave in the water, which climbed and feathered on his stomach, on the upstream side. When he was under the opposite bank a stone turned in earnest, and he went in. He came up, shouting with laughter, and made out loud a remark which has since become a classic in my family, 'Thank God,' he said, 'I rolled up my sleeves.' He wrung out

106

everything as best he could, and dressed again in the wet clothes, and set off up the shoulder of Niakatjavelk. He was dry and warm again in half a mile. Less than a thousand feet took him over the snow line, and there, crawling on hands and knees, he came face to face with what seemed to be the summit of ambition. He met an ermine. They were both on all fours, so that there was a sort of equality about the encounter, especially as the ermine was higher up than he was. They looked at each other for a fifth of a second, without saying anything, and then the ermine vanished. He searched for it everywhere in vain, for the snow was only patchy. My father sat down on a dry rock, to eat his well-soaked luncheon of chocolate and rye bread.

"Life is such unutterable hell, solely because it is sometimes beautiful. If we could only be miserable all the time, if there could be no such things as love or beauty or faith or hope, if I could be absolutely certain that my love would never be returned: how much more simple life would be. One could plod through the Siberian salt-mines of existence without being bothered about happiness. Unfortunately the happiness is there. There is always the chance (about eight hundred and fifty to one) that another heart will come to mine. I can't help hoping, and keeping faith, and loving beauty. Quite frequently I am not so miserable as it would be wise to be. And there, for my poor father sitting on his boulder above the snow, was stark happiness beating at the gates.

"The boulder on which he was sitting had probably never been sat upon before. It was a hundred and fifty miles within the Arctic Circle, on a mountain five thousand feet high, looking down on a blue lake. The lake was so long that he could have sworn it sloped away at the ends, proving to the naked eye that the sweet earth was round. The railway line and the half-dozen houses of Abisko were hidden in the trees. The sun was warm on the boulder, blue on the snow, and his body tingled smooth from the spate water. His mouth watered for the chocolate, just behind the tip of his tongue.

"And yet, when he had eaten the chocolate—perhaps it was heavy on his stomach—there was the memory of the Troll. My father fell suddenly into a black mood, and began to think about the supernatural. Lapland was beautiful in the summer, with the sun sweeping around the horizon day and night, and the small tree leaves twinkling. It was not the sort of place for wicked things. But what about the winter? A picture of the Arctic night came before him, with the silence and the snow. Then the legendary wolves and bears snuffled at the far encampments, and the nameless winter spirits moved on their darkling courses. Lapland had always been associated with sorcery, even by Shakespeare. It was at the outskirts of the world that the Old Things accumulated, like driftwood around the edges of the sea. If one wanted to find a wise woman, one went to the rims of the Hebrides; on the coast of Brittany one sought the mass of St. Secaire. And what an outskirt Lapland was! It was an outskirt not only of Europe, but of civilization. It had no boundaries. The Lapps went with the reindeer, and where the reindeer were, was Lapland. Curiously indefinite region, suitable to the indefinite things. The Lapps were not Christians. What a fund of power they must have had behind them, to resist the march of mind. All through the missionary centuries they had held to something: something had stood behind them, a power against Christ. My father realized with a shock that he was living in the age of the reindeer, a period contiguous to the mammoth and the fossil.

"Well, this was not what he had come out to do. He dismissed the nightmares with an effort, got up from his boulder, and began the scramble back to his hotel. It was impossible that a professor from Abisko could become a troll.

"As my father was going in to dinner that evening the manageress stopped him in the hall.

" 'We have had a day so sad,' she said. 'The poor Dr. Professor has disappeared his wife. She has been missing since last night. The Dr. Professor is inconsolable.'

"My father then knew for certain that he had lost his reason.

"He went blindly to dinner, without making any answer, and began to eat a thick sour-cream soup that was taken cold with pepper and sugar. The professor was still sitting in his corner, a sandy-headed man with thick spectacles and a desolate expression. He was looking at my father, and my father, with a soup spoon halfway to his mouth, looked at him. You know that eye-to-eye recognition, when two people look deeply into each other's pupils, and burrow to the soul? It usually comes before love. I mean the clear, deep, milk-eyed recognition expressed by the poet Donne. Their eyebeams twisted and did thread their eyes upon a double string. My father recognized that the professor was a troll, and the professor recognized my father's recognition. Both of them knew that the professor had eaten his wife.

"My father put down his soup spoon, and the professor began to grow. The top of his head lifted and expanded, like a great loaf rising in an oven; his face went red and purple, and finally blue; the whole ungainly upperworks began to sway and topple toward the ceiling. My father looked about him. The other diners were eating unconcernedly. Nobody else could see it, and he was definitely mad at last. When he looked at the Troll again, the creature bowed. The enormous superstructure inclined itself toward him from the hips, and grinned seductively.

"My father got up from his table experimentally, and advanced toward the Troll, arranging his feet on the carpet with excessive care. He did not find it easy to walk, or to approach the monster, but it was a question of his reason. If he was mad, he was mad; and it was essential that he should come to grips with the thing, in order to make certain.

"He stood before it like a small boy, and held out his hand, saying, 'Good evening.'

" 'Ho! Ho!' said the Troll, 'little mannikin. And what shall I have for my supper tonight?'

"Then it held out its wizened furry paw and took my father by the hand.

"My father went straight out of the dining-room, walking on air. He found the manageress in the passage and held out his hand to her.

" 'I am afraid I have burned my hand,' he said. 'Do you think you could tie it up?'

"The manageress said, 'But it is a very bad burn. There are blisters all over the back. Of course, I will bind it up at once.

"He explained that he had burned it on one of the spirit lamps at the sideboard. He could scarcely conceal his delight. One cannot burn oneself by being insane.

" 'I saw you talking to the Dr. Professor,' said the manageress, as she was putting on the bandage. 'He is a sympathetic gentleman, is he not?'

"The relief about his sanity soon gave place to other troubles. The Troll had eaten its wife and given him a blister, but it had also made an unpleasant remark about its supper that evening. It proposed to eat my father. Now very few people can have been in a position to decide what to do when a troll earmarks them for its next meal. To begin with, although it was a tangible troll in two ways, it had been invisible to the other diners. This put my father in a difficult position. He could not, for instance, ask for protection. He could scarcely go to the manageress and say, 'Professor Skal is an odd kind of werewolf, ate his wife last night, and proposes to eat me this evening.' He would have found himself in a loony-bin at once. Besides, he was too proud to do this, and still too confused. Whatever the proofs and blisters, he did not find it easy to believe in professors that turned into trolls. He had lived in the normal world all his life, and, at his age, it was difficult to start learning afresh. It would have been quite easy for a baby, who was still coordinating the world, to cope with the troll situation: for my father, not. He kept trying to fit it in somewhere, without disturbing the universe. He kept telling himself that it was nonsense: one did not get eaten by professors. It was like having a fever, and telling oneself that it was all right, really, only a delirium, only something that would pass.

"There was that feeling on the one side, the desperate assertion of all the truths that he had learned so far, the tussle to keep the world from drifting, the brave but intimidated refusal to give in or to make a fool of himself.

"On the other side there was stark terror. However much one struggled to be merely deluded, or hitched up momentarily in an odd pocket of space-time, there was panic. There was the urge to go away as quickly as possible, to flee the dreadful Troll. Unfortunately the last train had left Abisko, and there was nowhere else to go.

"My father was not able to distinguish these trends of thought. For him they were at the time intricately muddled together. He was in a whirl. A proud man, and an agnostic, he stuck to his muddled guns alone. He was terribly afraid of the Troll, but he could not afford to admit its existence. All his mental processes remained hung up, whilst he talked on the terrace, in a state of suspended animation, with an American tourist who had come to Abisko to photograph the Midnight Sun.

"The American told my father that the Abisko railway was the northernmost electric railway in the world, that twelve trains passed through it every day traveling between Uppsala and Narvik, that the population of Abo was 12,000 in 1862, and that Gustavus Adolphus ascended the throne of Sweden in 1611. He also gave some facts about Greta Garbo.

"My father told the American that a dead baby was required for the mass of St. Secaire, that an elemental was a kind of mouth in space that sucked at you and tried to gulp you down, that homeopathic magic was practiced by the aborigines of Australia, and that a Lapland woman was careful at her confinement to have no knots or loops about her person, lest these should make the delivery difficult.

"The American, who had been looking at my father in a

112

strange way for some time, took offense at this and walked away; so that there was nothing for it but to go to bed.

"My father walked upstairs on will-power alone. His faculties seemed to have shrunk and confused themselves. He had to help himself with the banister. He seemed to be navigating himself by wireless, from a spot about a foot above his forehead. The issues that were involved had ceased to have any meaning, but he went on doggedly up the stairs, moved forward by pride and contrariety. It was physical fear that alienated him from his body, the same fear that he had felt as a boy, walking down long corridors to be beaten. He walked firmly up the stairs.

"Oddly enough, he went to sleep at once. He had climbed all day and been awake all night and suffered emotional extremes. Like a condemned man, who was to be hanged in the morning, my father gave the whole business up and went to sleep.

"He was woken at midnight exactly. He heard the American on the terrace below his window, explaining excitedly that there had been a cloud on the last two nights at 11:58, thus making it impossible to photograph the Midnight Sun. He heard the camera click.

"There seemed to be a sudden storm of hail and wind. It roared at his windowsill, and the window curtains lifted themselves taut, pointing horizontally into the room. The shriek and rattle of the tempest framed the window in a crescendo of growing sound, an increasing blizzard directed toward himself. A blue paw came over the sill.

"My father turned over and hid his head in the pillow. He could feel the doomed head dawning at the window and the eyes fixing themselves upon the small of his back. He could feel the places physically, about four inches apart. They itched. Or else the rest of his body itched, except those places. He could feel the creature growing into the room, glowing like ice, and giving off a storm. His mosquito curtains rose in its afflatus, uncovering him, leaving him defenseless. He was in such an ecstasy of terror that he almost enjoyed it. He was like a bather plunging for the first time into freezing water and unable to articulate. He was trying to yell, but all he could do was to throw a series of hooting noises from his paralyzed lungs. He became a part of the blizzard. The bedclothes were gone. He felt the Troll put out its hands.

"My father was an agnostic, but, like most idle men, he was not above having a bee in his bonnet. His favorite bee was the psychology of the Catholic Church. He was ready to talk for hours about psychoanalysis and the confession. His greatest discovery had been the rosary.

"The rosary, my father used to say, was intended solely as a factual occupation which calmed the lower centers of the mind. The automatic telling of the beads liberated the higher centers to meditate upon the mysteries. They were a sedative, like knitting or counting sheep. There was no better cure for insomnia than a rosary. For several years he had given up deep breathing or regular counting. When he was sleepless he lay on his back and told his beads, and there was a small rosary in the pocket of his pyjama coat.

"The Troll put out its hands, to take him around the waist. He became completely paralyzed, as if he had been winded. The Troll put its hands upon the beads.

"They met, the occult forces, in a clash above my father's heart. There was an explosion, he said, a quick creation of power. Positive and negative. A flash, a beam. Something like the splutter with which the antenna of a tram meets its overhead wires again, when it is being changed about.

"The Troll made a high squealing noise, like a crab being boiled, and began rapidly to dwindle in size. It dropped my father and turned about, and ran wailing, as if it had been terribly burned, for one window. Its color waned as its size decreased. It was one of those air-toys now, that expire with a piercing whistle. It scrambled over the windowsill, scarcely larger than a little child, and sagging visibly.

"My father leaped out of bed and followed it to the window. He saw it drop on the terrace like a toad, gather itself together, stumble off, staggering and whistling like a bat, down the valley of the Abiskojokk.

"My father fainted.

"In the morning the manageress said, 'There has been such a terrible tragedy. The poor Dr. Professor was found this morning in the lake. The worry about his wife had certainly unhinged his mind.'

"A subscription for the wreath was started by the American, to which my father subscribed five shillings; and the body was shipped off next morning, on one of the twelve trains that travel between Uppsala and Narvik every day."

The Man

"Come on, Nicky. Rouse out. Stir your stumps."

The handsome boy, lounging, all knees, in the cheap arm-chair, his forehead on his hands, his elbows on the wooden arms, reading a library book by Ruby M. Ayres, looked up resentfully.

He said: "I want to finish this."

"Come along. You can finish it this evening. We've got to get a rabbit for Mrs. Creed."

He was seventeen. He hated the able, vigorous man of thirty, who was living with his mother. He did not know that he hated him. Nearly all the things which he felt seemed to be wrong, according to the people who surrounded him, so that, although his midriff hated the muscular man, and hated the arid chicken farm, and hated work, and hated his school, where he ought to be a prefect but was not, he hid these feelings and was ashamed of them and did not recognize them. For that matter, he hated himself. He wanted to slump in a chair and read himself away, into a less real world.

"Let me finish this chapter."

The man took the book off his knees and shut it firmly. He grinned at Nicky in a hearty way. He was one of those romp-ing ex-officers who thought in terms of a rough house in the mess, and of beer poured into the piano. He could do all the things that Nicky could not do—was a good carpenter, chicken farmer, football player.

"You'll read yourself blind."

"Oh, God! All right then."

The boy unfolded his awkward, despised body, which he loathed on the grounds that his ears stuck out, and hauled himself up.

"Shall I bring the gun?"

"If you like. We'll leave some of the holes open."

They collected the ferret, which Nicky would have handled gingerly, but which the man lifted at once—red eyes and needle teeth and stink and little claws. There was the bunch of rabbit nets, like string shopping bags, with their wooden pegs, and the old twelve-bore hammergun, single-barreled, which was all the farm could afford. Among the many things which kept the boy's heart in despair was poverty. He was extremely proud. He wanted to be rich, successful, admired, a gentleman like his forebears, a great painter, a lover. But what he had was the wooden bungalow to live in, and sickly chickens with lice, to pluck and clean unhandily, and, worst of the lot, the agonizing duty of delivering these corpses, during the holidays, at the doors of richer friends who had been poorer than his grandparents.

The three fox terriers yapped and frenzied their tails, the bitch revolving hers like a lamb. Nicky's mother, who was reading a library book, her main occupation, called out to bring two rabbits—so that they could have one for supper.

They passed through the ramshackle wire door into the wood.

The big trees had been cut down in the war. Now there were only saplings and undergrowth, a few silver birches and small poplars, and patches of bracken with curly shoots in spring, like bishops' croziers.

"We'll try the bury on Huggett's side."

He walked behind the man, on the narrow path between the fronds, in a muddle of adolescence. He believed himself bad, guilty and contemptible for feeling what he felt. He ought to work harder. He ought not to shirk cleaning out the chicken houses. He ought not to hate washing up. He ought to be more of a help to his adored mother—who was sacrificing so much to keep him at a public school. She had told him what a martyr, what an uncomplaining, protecting angel she was. He ought not to dislike and dread the efficient, masculine man who lived with her, and who did most of the work of the farm, helping to keep him at the school. Above all, at the school, he ought not to be in love with Peter Lea, who was fourteen. It was platonic—it was an empty cathedral of love and protection in his heart—but he accepted it as being shameful. In chapel, when there were lessons about David and Jonathan or innuendos in the sermon, he blushed and blushed.

His mother—the daughter of a general whose wife was bent on a K.C.B.—had been born in the civilization which existed before the Kinsey reports. She did not know what Dr. Schwarz has since declared, that two-thirds of the married women so far investigated are sexually frigid. She knew nothing about things like that. She was frigid.

When she had refused half a dozen proposals in most of the colonies where her father served, and had reached the age of thirty, her own mother had said to her one day: "Helen, do you think your father has got to keep you all your life?" At the end of one of those under-expressed, unforgivable, steely quarrels which daughters have with their mothers, she had said: "Very well, I will take the next man who asks me." And she had. Nicky's father, a rather artistic major who tried to write short stories and played the piano at regimental concerts, had not had his feelings considered in the matter.

After Nicky was born, his mother had refused to admit the Major to her bed, filling it with a family of fox terriers instead of a husband—the ancestors of the ones now present. She had become a hypochondriac, an omnivorous reader and a daydreamer. His father had taken to drink.

This was in the days when it was possible to get a judicial separation in England instead of a divorce, under the terms of which a husband, without being able to marry again, was made to provide his wife with a proportion of his income as alimony, and could never see her. Nicky's mother had chosen this form of attrition, and had got the separation on the grounds of cruelty. She was a strong-brained woman, and a good enough actress to win the judge.

Now, when she was forty-eight, she was sharing her chicken farm with the ex-officer of thirty. The latter was a remote cousin and, for all anybody knew, the relationship was as platonic as Nicky's was with Peter Lea.

The boy walked behind the broad shoulders, envying them or fearing them, noticing with a kind of mental wince the double column of the strong neck and the crisp, curling, fair hair, and the broad, red hands on the end of milk-white forearms. Among other things, the man was a better shot than he was, and this too was a cause for self-contempt.

120

The Man

At the bury, the untrained terriers dashed about and dug and barked, while the two pegged the nets over most of the holes, leaving a few with a clear run in front of them for shooting. It was a keen autumn day—a day for burning leaves, and for blue smoke rising stilly in sharp air. The tang of the afternoon remembered the slight frost of the morning. The Kentish woodlands, gently folding their horizons, were tawny with deciduous trees and patched in black with conifers.

The ferret, thrust into one of the holes, popped out again at once, head up, its pink nose sniffling. It poured off along the bank, quick, noiseless, unpredictable—a small round-bodied, perambulating waterfall of yellow fur, bouncing eccentrically. It vanished again.

There was the usual wait.

Nicky knew he would miss, if a rabbit bolted: he knew he would. At his best, he could only kill two out of three. The man hardly ever missed. As usual, he was being damned condescending, letting Nicky have the gun instead of himself— he, the leader man, who walked first along paths. The boy cocked the aged gun, arms tense, certain to make him poke. The man, a beautiful shot, would not have pulled the hammer back until the gun was at his shoulder, in the act of making fire.

"Damn. I think he's laid up."

He watched, the gun pointing downward, while the man listened from hole to hole, chirping between his lips, imitating the squeaking Teee of a dying animal.

"We'll have to put a bell on him. Or we could run him on a line. Oh hell, we've forgotten the spade."

He watched while the man, ingenious, energetic, able, made thumping noises with the palm of his hand on the earth to imitate the thump of a doe. He hated him consciously now.

He hated him for being with his lovely mother, for being better at everything in his mother's eyes than he was, for being the mainstay of the farm, for being good and patient at all the things he loathed himself—at mixing mash and carrying water and collecting eggs and mucking out the filthy, ammoniac pens. He hated him for being stupid, for not reading books or listening to the Proms on the wireless or seeing the tones and colors of pictures. He hated him as a Philistine, as a male, obstinate, powerful bull of successful flesh, who could thrash him with one hand tied behind his back.

The man lay down at Nicky's feet, with his ear to a rabbit hole. The gun was pointing directly at the back of his neck. I can pull this trigger, he thought. Nobody will know it was not an accident. I can say it caught in a twig. Boys are always supposed to be having accidents like that. I can just act dumb. They couldn't prove anything. And I am a minor. They can't hang you if you are a minor. I could actually pull it with a twig, or with the button on my coat sleeve. There was the time when Lance fired off his gun into the ground when loading it. They think all boys have accidents.

He put his finger around the trigger.

But he did not pull it.

He was not the operational type.

It would have surprised Nicky very much indeed to know that the man was fond of him and dumbly admired him. The latter was thinking, as he lay on his face chirping down the rabbit hole, with the twelve-bore pointing at the base of his skull, how brilliant Nicky was at school, and what a future he had in front of him, and that it was important to keep this cursed chicken farm on foot, to give the boy a chance.

The Black Rabbit

"I was a little boy," said the Professor, "when they brought me home to England, and I have loved my country all my life. Pansy can go to the continent if he likes, and I'm sure he enjoys it in his way, but in my case there is too little time for Britain. What is the use of seventy years? Life is intolerable if one loves one's fellow men: but for the selfish philosopher it is better than heaven, and far too short. I should like to go to Italy and commit a murder: I should like to go to Albania and shoot a mountaineer. I would have time to enjoy these things if I could live to be a thousand. Unfortunately I must sleep with my fathers. And I shall die before I have had time to learn the fringes of my own island.

"I don't know why I love the place. It takes the soul, some-how, with conviction. The shires have had to be my lovers, in the absence of anything else. Scotland, though without the fox, is heaven unadulterated: the greatest trial of my life took place in 1906, when I turned back from it at Penrith, com-pelled by the duty of a conscientious explorer, to sample the frilly miseries of the English Lakes. Gloucestershire burns in the affections as the country which combines the sports. You can hunt, fish and shoot there; and the beer is excellent; and architecture flourishes because the houses are made of the stone they stand on; and the tedium of too many trees and hedges vanishes; and man is rooted in his own earth, along with his stone walls and houses, growing out of the mother to which he will return. Trout in the Colne, hares on the top of Cleeve, the publican called Happy who keeps the Plough at Fairford, the love and courage of the civil wars: it is the history of England, twining about one's heart. Then there is the black list; renegade Sussex, unhealthy with trees and trippers and the bawling of the Belloc school; the pretty populated parts of Devonshire, self-conscious and debased; the Lake District itself; Surrey and the home counties, more suffering than sinful; and the environs of towns.

"It comes down to a question of sport. One can put it in hundreds of other ways, but the sport carries it best. Look at Sussex: where can one really hunt or fish? At Devonshire: the trout are small, and they chase the hedgeless stag. At the Lakes: mainly coarse fish and whited sepulchres like John Peel. At the home counties and the towns—well, I mean to say! Look at the anemic, miserable, myriad faces of the London streets. I was last forced to go there in 1907, but refused to stay the night. You could diagnose their horror at a glance. It was the lack of sport.

"Talking of sport, I shall tell you of an interview which I had when I was a boy of twelve. I was learning to fish, in one of the counties on my black list, in a river four feet broad, where nobody troubled to suspect the trout. He was a beauty if he was half-a-pound.

"It was a stream in a weald country, running a wooded valley. You could see a stone farmhouse, and an oasthouse, and an obelisk on the hill. The stream was overgrown, like a covered wagon, and you fished it by wading upstream in bare legs, casting a worm before you. It was like hockey. You could not afford to raise your rod above your shoulder, and spent most of the time disentangling it from the overhanging twigs. You lived for your rod-point, navigating it between the bushes, and dangled the writhing worm in the puddles below the ripples, and fought the four-inch trouts with a heart bounding to your mouth. You can imagine that it was heaven to a boy.

"It was heaven, and I was mad on being a sportsman, but I had a boy's perceptions. Everybody remembers the first rabbit they ever half-killed, and the first bright, leaping fish, and the fearful eye of the wounded bird, still cocking its snaky head, and the screaming hare. All forms of sport are horrible at first. You blood the young entry with the stinking smears of a mangled fox, and, if the child is at all sensitive, he spends the next ten minutes screaming on the ground. You make your youngster thread his own worms, and he shudders, face averted, over the oozing wriggler with its gummy exudations. You make him disgorge and kill his own fish, and he fears to hold them tight, and starts back from them as they flutter. You leave him to kill his back-broken rabbit, with its starting eyes, and he kicks at it, and looks for inadequate twigs to hit it with, fearing to touch it, hating it for being hurt.

"I loathed killing things, and yet I wanted to kill them. I trembled with lust for those half-pound trout, when I was on the point of catching them, and when I had caught them I was dismayed. I shuddered at knocking them on the head, had to avert my consciousness, and invented a convenient theory that it was kinder to let them suffocate. I wonder what it was. It may have been the fear of death.

"I was a thoughtful boy, and talked to keepers and such-like. A gillie, the previous season, had made me hold a salmon-rod in my right hand, bent double in the proper running position, with the lure between the finger and thumb of my left. He made me do it, to feel the pull exerted on a fish. It was very little, a question of a pound or so. Even allowing for the buoyancy which would make a fish lighter in water (and, at that age, I forgot to allow for this), it seemed quite inadequate to tire a heavy salmon so quickly. It was a dreadful thought that these precious shark-backed monsters might be killed by slow attrition, by an agony worse than toothache, at the agonizing hook. And then one thought of the hard-hit partridges, with the lead shot in their entrails, going gangrenous. Perhaps the hunted foxes were the worst thought of all. There was a hunt with the Grafton under Frank Beris, on the 9th of November, 1870, when a fox from Bucknells took them for an hour and ten minutes at best pace, ran into a front door, down a passage to the back kitchen, and was killed under the table. Think of the wild creature, shooting his last bolt, running into the den of his hereditary enemies for sanctuary. That sort of thing was by no means a rare occurrence. I never was fool enough to say that a fox enjoyed being hunted, or needed to be. A fox from Easton Neston Gardens, in 1888, was run till he could not stand, and lay down in a railway cutting. Two trains came past him, but he did not move. Two plate-layers came and hit him with their caps, until he began to climb the embankment. Halfway up, he lay down again, and a whip was sent to stir him to the road. At last he was brought out, and staggered away, and the hounds knocked him over at a walk.

"If you like fishing for pike with live bait, the best way is to stick two or three hooks firmly into the body of a live roach or perch, and let it swim away on the end of your trace. The pain usually kills it in a few minutes, but before that its struggles may have attracted the attention of a pike, which will finally be finished by hitting it on the head. I understand that a stag's throat is cut, if he does not choose the alternative of being drowned. In killing a pig, you make a slight incision between the shoulder and the neck, and pry about with a long knife in order to reach the heart. A skilful butcher can reach it at the first or second thrust. Shrimps make a thin noise, between a whistle and the sing of a kettle, while they are being boiled alive.

"But I was telling you about my interview. It happened on a summer day, with the mayfly going up and down in their exciting nuptials, and the cattle flicking their tails, and the rich English countryside seeming to roll over on its back and offer its body to the sun. There was a hawk by the oasthouse, hanging in the blue air with a lazy motion, and two little trouts lay on the bank above me, with their rosy spots unfaded.

"As a general rule I used to get so wrapped up in the particular puddle I was fishing that the passage of two hours would find me scarcely a hundred yards along the stream. On this day, however, I was determined to penetrate to our boundary: a hazy country, undiscovered, about a mile beyond the farm.

"I don't know when I began to feel uncomfortable. One never met anybody, even by the farm, but I suppose the mere sight of the buildings must have been company. They vanished, as you wended up the stream.

"I began to feel self-conscious, separated from myself. My movements became odd to me, in this deserted valley. Lonely is a word used by romantics to describe their form of life; as such, it is inadequate to express my oddness. I was not lonely, but alone. Absolutely alone: you must think about that. I felt cut off from humanity, surrounded only by those silent, sunny meadows and the wooded slopes. It was not exactly that they watched me. They were content to surround me, standing at ease. I felt that my movements were foreign and clumsy and overlooked.

"That was the first stage; but I wanted to rush the boundary and imagined all sorts of better pools in front.

"After a time I began to feel frightened. It seemed ridiculous and intrusive to be fishing, and I was ashamed of my dead fish. The rod seemed silly, and there was an enmity about. But I had set myself on doing the thing, and I was not going to be a baby. I went on, fishing quickly and without interest, up the valley.

"In a way it came soon, for there was only a mile in which it could come, but in another way it was a development, a gradual accumulation to the bend. The rivulet took a turn there, and the woody hills came in, and even the obelisk had vanished. It was like stepping out of things, if you understand me: out of mankind, through looking-glasses, however you like to put it. There were two little fields by the river and then nothing but a wood, a dead end. And one was around the turn, so that there was nothing behind one either, only the trees. One had stepped into it, and the trap had closed. I knew the chestnuts were shutting silently behind me. There was a black rabbit in the field.

"The ancients worshipped Pan, but not like Mr. Kenneth Grahame. Panic was the noun derived from his name. He was the god of nature. He was the god who had arranged that women should have children in the way they do. He was the god whose tigers clawed gaunt cattle in India, whose subjects died of alligators or festering wounds or cancer; it did not matter of what. He was the god of the animals, to which we humans are a branch. He preserved the balance of nature. He preserved us, like the pheasants of Euston. Shiva or Pan, it was the same thing: the destroyer and the preserver.

"The black rabbit turned my exploration into panic. It sat up, looking at me, waiting for me with its ears erect. The silence of the valley was extraordinary. None of the birds were singing. I watched at an open bend, with my head just over the steep bank of the stream. There was time to steal away.

"When I turned I nearly jumped out of my skin. There was a keeper standing on the bank behind me. The first keeper I knew had told me that he liked to have a black rabbit at the buries; because if it disappeared he could tell at a glance whether he was being poached. I thought of this and looked back at the rabbit, but it was gone. Then I looked at the strange man, whom I had never seen before.

"I can't describe his face to you. It was neither kind nor cruel, or perhaps it would be truer to say that it was both. There was the pike's ironic mouth, bony and predatory; but its strength had a good-humor about it, and there were crow's-feet around the eyes. He stood looking down at me, with his hammergun over the crook of his arm, in great hairy stockings and cracked boots, with ankle-straps around the top of them.

"I knew who he was at once, but his expression cured my terror. I remained afraid of him, a deferential boy trying to propitiate the unpredictable, but not actively panic-stricken: just very small and polite. I gave him my stippled fish; and he took them in a capable paw, inclining his head, and stowed them in his poacher's pocket. His hands were brown, horny, padded, crooking inward at the fingers. The two trouts nestled quite easily in the one palm, side by side. He inclined his head, and stowed them, and sat down cross-legged on the bank, with his gun across his knees.

"He talked to me. At first I played up to him, asking pedantic questions, trying to keep him in a good humor, trying to be an intelligent listener, sucking up to him like a child at school. He was as terrible as a schoolmaster of those days and as distinct a species.

"It was only for a few moments. Nobody can be terrible who is talking truth; and boys distinguish it. He talked to me about the world: not the human world, with its intellectual cross-purposes, but the animal one. He talked about the strange toes of the crested grebe, and the red teeth of the merganzer, and grouse disease, and furunculosis, and scent, and charges of shot, and the old days of horsehair instead of gut, and the generation of the eel, and adders swallowing their young, and woodcock carrying them, and whether flies settle on the ceiling, and the spawning of salmon, and what a fish can see. It was a fascinating lecture. I was listening soon, without a trace of flunkeyism, charmed to my heart. If I could remember all he said about the ultra-red and ultra-violet I should be the greatest dry-fly fisherman alive. Perhaps the best joy he gave me was a simple one, which can be shared by any ignorant marksman. He broke his gun for me and made me look up the barrel, which was clean. About a cartridge-length from the hammer there were the two black rings which are believed by most people to indicate the place where a special groove for the cartridge ends. I believed that there was a socket for the cartridge, slightly wider than the proper barrel and of more or less unproofed steel. He made me investigate this socket with my finger, and then with a pencil. A simple investigation, but for a small boy it was a surprise.

"I told him in my turn the things I had discovered. He must have known them, but he listened with interest. We talked about the drumming of snipe. I told him of my hopes and fears. I told him that I hated killing fish, and felt sorry for them dead that had been so lively in the water.

"He said: 'The Colne flows through the fields of Gloucestershire. The cuckoo speaks to you all day, and dreams over the audible water. He lies under the far bank, under the alder-tree, and the March browns are sailing their Armadas. The river is clean water and quick, bubbling and swirling between the cresses, full of ephemerids and nymphs and shrimps. The sun sparkles on the crystal run. You can see the stones at the bottom, in the slow shallows, and a stoat has run across that sheep-wire that acts as a suspension bridge. He lost his balance twice, and turned around on it like a monkey, with anxious squeaks, and has scuttled off between your legs as if you were an inanimate object. Listen to that cart-horse further down the river. He has been an ardent bather from his youth, and takes his dip three times a sunny day, rolling on his back with a surprised expression. The swallows are dipping and the sun is low. Look at the trout, how they are going mad at the hatch, butting at them shoulder to shoulder. Do you think we could reach the big fellow under the alder, in spite of the ripple between us that will drag the fly, so casting it that it will hang for just one second over his brown nose, before the drag begins?'

" 'But isn't it cruel?' I asked.

"He only said: 'The Colne is clear, and runs over the cresses.'

"He said: 'We are in the stubble now, and we've got them where they ought to be. Hark to them cheeping, with their heads up. Look at that covey on the right, going straight away from him like chips from a sharpened pencil, and see his gun come up to throw out its fingers of smoke before the bang, and look at the two birds turning and overtipping in a flutter of exploded feathers. Here is the bang now, and the smoke hangs in the September air, and the black Labrador is working. Hie lost! Hie lost! We are behind the hedge for a drive, kneeling on one knee, and the first covey has come over two guns to the left, rising scarcely two feet off the ground and skimming the hedges at fifty miles an hour. He has missed them with both barrels, as well he might. And here is the second covey over the higher part, forty of them at least. The first gun has turned them, missing with both silent pointers of smoke, and the second gun has browned them with the same result, and the third gun is firing, but there is no time to attend to him. They are overhead, high and scattered, like a handful of thrown clods. The first barrel turns the picked bird over, in a somersault, stone-dead, and the second brings another down from the vertical, a runner that can't go far: the first left and right of the season!'

" 'But don't they suffer?' I asked.

"He only said: 'There is a ground-mist in the morning, with a tang in the air, and hundreds of well-shaped September clouds.'

"He said: 'It is four in the morning, and we are after duck.

What a levee it was in the black darkness, with our bleary eyes and unshaven chins, drinking rum and coffee before the dawn. And here we are in the night light, early enough to be sure that nothing will have come before us. In half an hour they will be here, a stately flight of four which we shall hear but scarcely see, and miss with both barrels. The bats will still be hawking in the early dim, and a big dragonfly rattles its wings in the reeds. Here they are again: unbirdlike, smooth, purposeful, apparently slow. The snake-neck stretches out with a little knout at the end of it: sighted on a certainty. Now they are coming fast, and there is a fusillade all around the water, and the gun is hot as quick as you can load, and he goes into the water-lilies with a swash, a long shot, stone-dead.'

"I said. 'But it must be agony.'

"He only answered: "The last duck is circling high, with the bright dawn tinting his breasting feathers so that he looks like a pochard. The wee viper-knot of his head turns this way and that, directly above us, in anxious curiosity.'

" 'Look here,' I said. 'What about the hunted fox?'

" 'Hounds are running,' he said, 'with a cry that rings through the woods. Hark to them chiming to it, and the huntsman's horn. Whilst the field was coffee-housing by the bridle-gate we edged away to the right, and that is our line. We feel like going, this winter morning. Here is a gate, which we can open with plenty of time, and now we are on firm pasture, with the fences ahead. The first is a far-side ditch, which is meat and drink to us, however wide and deep it is. The second is a bullfinch, taken at a scramble, with our hat over our eyes. Now the valley dips below us, and we can

135

count the fences ahead, half a dozen blue bars stretching into the distance at our feet. The fields are emeralds between them and the high clouds hang over, and the twigs will crackle.'

"I said: 'They will tear him to pieces.'

"He said: 'They are matched in mouth like bells.'

" 'Look at the slatey water,' he said, 'with a scum of bubbles floating down the ripple. You would think it was a hopeless day for salmon, but with fish you never know. We have given up hope and are casting mechanically, with the wind behind us, taking pleasure in the cast itself. Hard back and gently forward; let it take itself. It is good to cast straight, with a huge Mar Lodge plopping at the end of a sizzle of straight gut, if there isn't a fish in the world. The gillie is smoking his pipe on a game-bag, watching us with friendly interest and commiseration. He has few hopes from the color of the water, but our tenacity gives him pleasure. There was a fish leaped ten minutes ago, a vertical monster suddenly displaying his belly and spread gills, and anybody but a fool would give it up. But he has been leaping there at intervals all day, and they may not be running. Perhaps it is something else. Hence the Mar Lodge. This is the sixth lure we have tried to tempt him with, more to pass the time than anything else. We started with a trout fly, a claret and teal. Try him for the last time with this black contrivance, that had never taken a fish before. It's as big as a boat-hook, pitch-black, with silver around the body. None but a lunatic salmon would take it, and nobody but a lunatic would make the offer, but perhaps we are both mad. And, by God, it has got him. Wow! says the gillie, and is on his feet. Hold him for dear life. Look at the line cutting the water, cruising the pool like a wire

136

cutting cheese. Now look collectedly at your wrist-watch and note the time. We take a pride in killing them under ten minutes. Look out, you will have to give in to him: but grudgingly, only by a few turns. We'll take him for a saunter down the stream. Five minutes and we haven't had a sight of him, not even a rusty flash in the water. Now he's taking the law into his own hands, and we've got to follow him up the bank. Never mind; go with him, it will tire him out. Look out! He is going to leap. There he goes, with a flash and a flurry. Drop your rod-point as he smacks in on his side, and tighten up, and almost before you're ready he's out again. Three leaps like fury, in quick succession. What a noise he makes! I should judge him at fourteen pounds. Now he's beginning to tire; now we've got him on the hip. Don't be a genteel angler and fiddle with him for forty minutes. Bring him in now, with a ruthless hand. Tell that gillie to drop the gaff. We aren't going to be a gentleman. Now feel for it with your left hand, bending at the knees, with the rod high above your head in the right. Here he is below us, beginning to turn on his side; but he catches his first glimpse as we hover above him, and goes off like a flash. All right, my beauty, you can go once around the pool. Bring him around in a circle and navigate him to your feet. As you step down he will be off again, but this time the circle is only a few yards. Now we've got him in a little bay, and he lies burrowing at the bank, which makes us fear for our gut. Lay the gaff along his side quite gently. No hacking and snatching. Now is the time. Everything depends on this. Now for the firm, piercing draw. And here you are, staggering up the bank, with fourteen pounds of silver-and-black flapping on the end of your gaff-handle!'

"I said: 'Poor fish!'

" 'Yes,' said the Keeper Pan, nodding his head, 'but in Scotland the line cuts the water, like a wire cutting cheese.' "

Kin to Love

The defense talked about epilepsy, moral responsibility, and whether he understood the nature and quality of his act. Is anybody responsible for anything? You can only go by common sense.

He was a handsome boy of twenty-one, a Rudolph Valentino to look at. He did not follow the conventions which are expected to go with masculine beauty in fiction. He was not a gigolo, or vain, or self-satisfied, and did not trade on his good looks. He thought his personal appearance effeminate, in fact, and spent part of his time trying to alter it. He used solid brilliantine, in the effort to flatten the natural wave of his fair hair. He did exercises for two hours every day with an elastic chest-expander. He avoided his eyes in mirrors, being reluctant to look at himself. He was fascinated by guns and daggers, which he associated with virility. He was desperately, ashamedly, confusedly sexual.

He was undependable about money, and had been on probation for theft. They called him a delinquent.

His name was Edward Norvic, an orphan. His few friends called him Rudy, which he hated. Although he had yellow hair, he had long, black eyelashes which fanned his cheeks. In shape and figure he looked like Donatello's statue of the adolescent David, or was it Perseus? He was sometimes pursued by middle-aged scoutmasters or shifty clergymen, and had more than once succumbed to them, to his grief, although his nature was fiercely heterosexual. About this, as about money, he was not reliable. He deplored his weakness. He chased females persistently, not confidently, unaware of his attractions, so that his uncertainty made him unsuccessful and furtive in following the pursuit.

If he was a Valentino at all, he was a secretive, lonely, introverted specimen of the type, who brooded about sex and despised it and dreaded his lusts.

The Norvics who had adopted him—an elderly couple—had been kind and nonconformist, giving him love and punishment, so that the two were mixed in his mind. This was the trouble. Their love for the good part of him was fused with repression for what they thought the bad part. If they had been unpleasant and loveless people, he could have felt contempt for their standards and could have defied their sanctions. But they loved him, and he loved them, so he accepted their standards while failing to live up to them. His sexual rigor, which might have taken and given so much pleasure, was contorted by morals foreign to his nature—morals which he accepted because they came with affection. He was affectionate himself. He was not clever or artistic or well-educated. His levels were more or less those of Garth in the strip cartoons of the *Daily Mirror*. He was neither strong nor weak, though he thought himself weak. He did not see that he failed his commandments because they were too high for him. All he knew was that he failed them. So he was driven to do it secretly. He had been given a conscience. He was prim.

None of these facts was of importance to the judge at the

140

trial, because they were not covered by the McNaughton Rules. The nearest cliché for the legal mind turned out to be that he was "a moral defective."

On the day of the murder, Norvic rode his racing-type pedal cycle to the woods near Fullerton in the afternoon. It was his half-day holiday.

He was armed with a spring knife or stiletto, expensively bought from a friend in the merchant navy who had got it in Naples, and with an out-of-date Holland revolver which had belonged to a police officer in India thirty years before. It had three rounds of modern ammunition in its six chambers. The weapons were his fetish.

He did not go to the woods with a conscious purpose. Or rather, he had two separate purposes, and was not fully aware of either of them. Even this is not quite accurate. His official purpose was to pass the time and for exercise, woodcraft, or a long walk during which he would probably imagine himself a commando leader, or a parachutist, or perhaps some sort of gangster or federal agent—in any case, an armed and athletic person without inhibitions. His unconscious hope, which is perhaps the main hope of most people aged twenty-one, most of the time, was to meet, examine, meditate upon and if possible accost females. These he wished to violate, not fondle. At the trial, they argued about knowing the difference between right and wrong. The point which everybody missed was that it was this knowledge which made him homicidal. The ferocity of his sex was due to believing too much in right and wrong. He thought it was wrong to fondle women, so he had to rape them. He was a plugged volcano which could only erupt by violence. He had accepted, but could not observe, the standards of the class which had adopted him.

He had had five women in his life, three of them minors, with clumsy, ungentle, uncomprehending, selfish acquisition, followed by shame. But it had been with their consent. He had thrillingly beaten one of them with a willow stick.

He was kind to animals. His cruelty was associated with sex. Apart from this, he was not particularly good and not particularly bad—a confused, unattractive youth, with abnormal but fairly common instincts, which he had not selected for himself—an explosive mixture well tamped by taboos which made them more explosive—a stupid and ordinary mind of little charm or promise—a lout. But he had never murdered anybody before, and he might never have murdered anybody again. On the whole, he was not unlike his fellow men. His more repellent features were the lies, willfulness and despotic selfishness common to children of six years old. His mental age was not much higher.

It was a sparkling day in the early summer, the tree leaves virgin green, with their egg-shaped sun-specks dancing on the rather shabby undergrowth of woods which were too close to a successful watering-place—too much frequented by lovers, trippers and the litter-makers of holiday resorts. It was a "beauty spot."

He locked his bicycle and left it in a ditch beside a rustic stile. He sauntered and imagined among verdant trees, striving confusedly with all the sinful lusts of the flesh. His imaginations, like Boswell's at the same age, were of the seraglio. Most people are like Boswell, only they don't say so.

Mrs. Evans, the district nurse, was a middle-aged or elderly Welsh widow with a faint moustache. She was shaped like a beer barrel with bow legs, or perhaps like a Queen Anne bureau—a short, stout, warm-hearted body of tireless good hope and not much intelligence, who bicycled through sun or rain or snow or thunder, year in and year out, from confinement to confinement, in a personal aura of kindness and help. Like many fat people, she had small feet on which she could move at British Legion whist-drives-and-dances with wonderful lightness and grace. Like many ugly or at least homely women, she was feminine and modest and dainty in her person. She had knickknacks in her small, cozy, clean parlor— china ornaments bearing the arms of Bournemouth or Margate, and earthenware porringers in brown and green and biscuit-color with admonitions written on them, such as Tak' Anither Drap o'Tay, or Set Ye Down And Bide A Wee.

She used to adore her husband, who had been devoted to her, but they had been childless. When the husband died, seven years before, he had left her the cottage in which she lived alone—in which she sustained herself with a nice chop or a cheering cup of Camp Coffee or some Ovaltine and sugar biscuits, sleeping sound and living decently, warmed at evening by the merry gas fire after the drag of her daily round, companied by a Persian cat.

She was afraid of what she anxiously called Doggies, though she tried to be polite to them. The ones who detected this weakness treated her with contempt and animosity, as if she were a postman, while the ones who liked her tried to jump up—an approach which she believed to be menacing.

She had an amethyst brooch in the shape of a lucky spider.

Mrs. Evans was wheeling her battered cycle through the woodland path on a shortcut to Fairbourne, where she had a case of paralysis, an old-age pensioner. There was nothing she could do for the old man except see that he was kept clean and comfortable, visiting him once a week. They were cronies. He called her Matty.

She was thinking about various subjects, none of which were connected with physical passion. They were: whether she would have a poached egg or a tin of baked herrings for her tea, whether her sister in Aberystwyth could be persuaded to come to Fullerton for her annual holiday, whether she had better stop at the doctor's to get more morphia for Mrs. Norton, whether the sea was really blue or how blue on the Isle of Capree, and if you could get fresh butter there, why as was commonly said it should be assumed that the earth went around the sun when it obviously did not move, whether she had remembered to leave the back window open for the cat, and what a pity it was that the bluebells were all broken or pulled up by the trippers who visited Fairbourne-Church-in-the-Woods.

When she heard the man walking behind her, she was not disturbed.

There were lovers all over the place hereabouts, and her heart warmed to them. Why not, poor things? They were young and spring was still in the air. She knew the quotation about a young man's fancy and one of her favorite statements, was It Is Love that Makes the World Go Round. Such had been her experience with Mr. Evans. She plodded on sturdily with her bicycle, rolling slightly on the bandy legs.

But the footsteps continued, not getting nearer or further. She looked over her shoulder.

Except for dogs—and this was only due to the repulsion of a cat lover—Mrs. Evans had never been afraid of anything outside herself. She was a qualified nurse for whom spurting arteries and hideous diseases and the butchery of surgeons held no terrors. She could cope with fits and hysterics and drunks and even lunatics, for she had once worked in a private asylum for four months. But this time it was not outside herself—it was not a "patient." It was personal to herself, to her femininity, to the delicacy of her womanhood. Young people are surprised to learn, and unwilling to believe, that even plump, elderly and uncomely women may still think of themselves as female. It is difficult and rather ludicrous to realize that the fat old things we meet may have remained what they always were inside—may have remained modest virgins, or tender dreamers, or teasing flirts whose airy graces have been betrayed only by the Judas of the body.

Mrs. Evans began to run, thrusting her bicycle through the long grass beside the path, which was too thick for cycling.

Edward Norvic began to run too.

If she had gone on walking, he would have walked as well. But, by the act of flight, she had taken on the role of a quarry, which forced him to be the hunter. He had been "setting" her before. Shooting dogs—pointers for instance—will stand rigid for ages, setting a cat, but when the cat runs they have to run too. While she walked, she had been a stout district nurse. When she ran, she was a woman, the pursued. She had made herself his prey, and that made him the captor. She had lost her individuality and become a sex. The very way she ran, the actual action of her haunches and slope of her shoulders in the dowdy uniform reminded him of every Eve since

Adam, jerking the arrow of his loins. He had to run, as if they were tied together. He had to capture her, to pounce, to seize, embrace, subdue. He had no intention of killing her. He had to lay her for the burning mastery.

Mrs. Evans began to scream when he caught her. This was worse. This made him feel that she expected to be killed.

So he had to kill her.

They say that pity is akin to love. So is its opposite. Ferocity is even closer kin.

The condemned cell in that particular prison was separated from the main block. It stood in the yard by itself, a mean little building of two rooms and a narrow corridor. The prisoners spent exactly twenty-four hours in it, being brought at eight o'clock on one morning and hanged at eight o'clock the next. Convicts called it the Topping Shed.

The smaller or living-room was about sixteen feet square— the flimsy, institutional walls being of one brick thickness. Most of the north wall was taken up by a large window of frosted glass with bars and wire netting. There were two doors. One door was the entry from the yard. The other door—the exit—would open only once for every prisoner. Doomfully shut, foreboded, dodged by the eye, it dominated the shoddy, unloved chamber with a looming, belly-sinking blank. It was what you turned your mind away from.

And yet this room was in a way loved, when in use. When not in use, it was a bare, scrubbed cube, maintained by the Office of Works, with a floor of unstained boards. But for the customer, it was furnished. It was even furnished with a kind of rueful affection—an apologetic kindness, a wish to comfort. The governor himself would send across his own armchair. There were two stiff chairs for the warders of the death watch. There was a table for draughts or backgammon or games of cards. On the board floor there was a pathetic little drugget. The bed had clean sheets and blankets, as neat as a hospital. Indeed, it was the waiting-room for a lethal hospitality.

The warders who sat in the deadly room with Norvic were genuinely kind men, not like the thuggish jailers or policemen of fiction. They had fine-drawn, friendly smiling faces, paternal and ministering, like helpful nurses giving individual attention and support in a kind nursing home.

One of them always sat with his chair-back masking the door.

They talked their best.

Behind the door was a narrow, tiled corridor, like the approach to a public lavatory, scarcely a pace wide. Across this corridor, not along it, only a yard away, was the door to the other room. This was bigger, like a squash court or a gymnasium without apparatus. It was much higher than the cell and solidly built—the cell being, in fact, a kind of lean-to erected against its outer wall. There was no furniture whatever, except for two fixtures. One was a cast-iron girder padded with gray felt in the middle, from which there hung three ropes. The middle rope was leather-lined at the noose, which ran through a metal eye and was temporarily held open with pack-thread. The other two ropes were without nooses. The second fixture was the trapdoor underneath the girder. It was ten or twelve feet square and consisted of two wooden flaps hinged at the outer edges, just like the double doors of a barn laid flat instead of upright. On each flap there was a ring bolt. To each ring there was a stout cord. When not in use, these cords were neatly curled in circles—maritime-looking, shipshape and Bristol fashion. At present they were stretched at right angles to the hinges. They were for lifting the flaps again, after use. In the middle of the trap, a white circle was drawn in chalk, where the prisoner was to stand. On either side of it, crossing the trap at right angles, there was a loose safety-board, like the planks which plasterers and house-painters use. These were for the hangman and the two prison officers to stand on, when the time came, steadying themselves by holding the two spare ropes. The only other feature in the void, still, echoing gymnasium was the lever which released the trap. It stood from the floor like a lever in a railway signal box, only smaller, or like the high hand-brake of an old-fashioned car.

Such was the Topping Shed: a living-room and a dying-room was all it had.

The prison governor was a miniature Santa Claus, without the whiskers. Pink-cheeked and twinkling, five and a half feet high, looking healthier and younger than his nearly sixty years, he loved the country prison. It was not as a prison that he loved it, but as a place which he had made better—a place which his optimism and kindness had improved to the very limit allowed by reasonable deterrence. The hideousness of man was responsible for the hideousness of jails, but the governor had put his faith in man and done his best for both of them. The gardens were looked after by volunteer labor among the convicts, and lovingly looked after. With a strange and touching sort of pride they had trimmed the name of the prison in clipped letters along the box borders of the paths. The Victorian façades had all sorts of creepers and potted

plants and geraniums and vegetable fancies. The sills of the
barred windows were color-washed to cheer them up. The
old-fashioned cells were neat, centrally heated, with good
mattresses and blankets, a chamberpot and three library
books each week. For those who behaved themselves—which
was nearly all of them—there was a recreation room for an
hour and a half every evening, with a dart board and a radio.
Nor were they segregated all day. In the summer they might
be breaking stones in the yard, in the winter chopping kind-
ling wood in a big shed—but in company, and not in strict
silence. The water of the shower baths was really hot, the
cooking plainly good on excellent Aga cookers. In the prison
church there was not one bar or bolt or handcuff. For many
years a local scallywag had habitually broken a shop window
every Christmas Eve, proceeding at once to the police station
under his own power, to give himself up. He did it for his
winter holiday, and for the turkey dinner on Christmas
Day.

Through this home—for it was a home, with a sort of
family feeling and *esprit de corps* of its own—the sprightly,
Dickensian governor moved with proprietorship, rubbing his
soft hands together and being kind. He was not weak or
cranky, and nobody took advantage of him. At a certain line,
he could be as firm as rock.

He was married to a pippin who was as apple-cheeked as
he was himself, with a grown-up family. He was ashamed of
being the overlord among men whose liberty had been taken
from them. When he conducted visitors over the prison, he
made nervous, propitiatory little jokes about dungeons and
torture chambers and Madame Tussaud's. He was fond of
Gilbert and Sullivan operas. If he and his wife had been birds,

they would have been budgerigars, twittering merrily in a clean cage.

He had never had an execution before.

At two minutes to eight, the governor, the chaplain, the doctor, the hangman and two warders opened the outer door of the living-room.

The death watch stood up. Edward Norvic stood up. It would take ninety seconds.

The governor patted Edward Norvic, pressing his arm with warmth and tenderness and encouragement. He had seen to it that he was "given something" before his breakfast. The chaplain began to read. The hangman pinioned the prisoner. The paling warders sustained themselves in military fashion, assuming faces of wood.

Edward Norvic found that there were no bones in his legs: instead, soda water. He was shaking tremendously, but not with fear. He observed himself from outside, independently shaking. They slipped the bag over his head.

The door was opened.

The door to the other room, to the operating room, was open already. Through it they wheeled or led or hustled or companied the cooperating patient, docile to his fatal operation.

Quickly on the trapdoor, so that his despairing blindfold, nuzzling the new room avidly for a last lookful of life, might not through linen see one detail. Quickly the ready noose over his hooded dumbness, and the straps around his legs for walking never more to be needed. Quickly the governor's signal and the heave on the standing lever.

The trap fell open with a sickening thud, unmasking the whitewashed walls of the pit, twelve feet square and deep. If the neck broke, if the rope twanged, both sounds were swallowed by the thundering, bouncing trap. The already stretched cord did not creak. It swayed and revolved. Nothing was to be seen of Edward Norvic.

The first thing was to get everybody out of the place. Such were the instructions. The governor began to shepherd them through the door, pushing them in the small of the back, saying, "Out, out!" They hurried, jostling in the narrow doorway. They glanced, each one, but only the flash of a glance, into the white Hell which had opened under them as they passed it. The rope thrilled and swung.

In the fresh air, with dry mouths and the blood drained from their temples, they dispersed or split into groups. The chaplain went to his office. The governor walked up and down with the doctor. The hangman paired with the chief warder. The others stood about at hand. Cigarettes were lighted, a necessary relaxation of rules. They tried with painful levity to think of dirty stories. They had to keep it up for thirty minutes.

The dirty stories, in the clear sunlight of the high-walled, empty yard, were better than speculation. They were better than wondering why, if hanging is supposed to be so instantaneous an exit, the now priapic corpse should need a half-hour on the gallows—better than wondering why, even at the post mortem, the doctor's first duty might be to make a small incision, and cut the spinal cord. It was better than wondering why an ill-topped man might sometimes snore, and hearts, though hanged, beat on.

When the allotted time was over and the pit had been revisited—the govenor and the doctor climbing down first—when life had been pronounced extinct and the subsequent machinery set in motion—when nothing knowable was left of the mind of Edward Norvic, the governor went back to his own house.

There, in the kitchen, as he had hoped and known she would be, was his wife in her dressing gown, making coffee. She put her soft arms around his neck. He held her tight. He conducted her upstairs, silently, urgently, pleading

The Father Christmas face, in the act of orgasm, bore much the same expression of agony and congestion as the dead boy's profile wore, cooling in the mortuary.

Soft Voices at Passenham

The Professor said: "Very few people ever see ghosts, because they are localized. Now Passenham is a good locality for ghosts, near Stony Stratford. They have more ghosts there than ratepayers."

"All these supernatural stories," said the Countess coldly, "boil down to hearsay in the end. Even the Holy Ghost has always struck me as being a great deal less definite than the other members of the Trinity. Have you ever seen one of the creatures yourself?"

"At Passenham I attended a sort of concert with several of them. Ghosts are fond of music, and will go anywhere to hear it."

"Did you actually see one?"

"No," replied the Professor with reluctance.

"I suppose you'll have to tell the story if your mind is set on it."

"I don't tell stories to amuse myself," said the Professor in dignified tones.

"Of course you do, Jacky. Don't be so pompous. You know perfectly well that you consider nobody's interests in that matter except your own. And, what is more, you make them up as you go along."

The Professor smiled a pleased smile.

153

"It is the creative urge," he said. "But this one is deadly true."

"I believe you."

"Why, of course it's true. Passenham is a real place. You can look it up in any map of the shire. How could I invent stories about a real place? For that matter, you can go there and see for yourself."

"Thank you for nothing," said the Countess. "Who wants to go and see a ghost, anyway? Horrid creatures smelling of mold!"

"Mold," repeated the Professor with relish. "Mold. Well may you say mold. It is not only music that ghosts are fond of, but also mist. Music and mist. Damp. Humidity. The watery air that makes things go moldy: go soft and cold and wet and furry. Toadstools, you know, and that steeped pervasive cellar air, and the bleached delicate green-blue fur between the chinks. The silent damp rots their bodies away to bones, and I suppose they need the same thing to build them up again before they walk. There is something solid about humidity, something ectoplasmic with which to compose a soft and putrid body visible to men."

"I think you're horrid," said the Countess.

"I was trying to explain about Passenham," explained the Professor. "It lies low and flat, on the banks of the Ouse. The Ouse is a very haunted stream really, as you can imagine from its name. Silent, green and slimy, it goes slow and cold through the flooded winter landscape: bearing with it the bodies of drowned maidens, goggle-eyed in midwater, attended by sluggish perch and muddy roach and a few staring, garbage-eating trout. The ironic pike lie frozen in the water, and the stream itself scarcely seems to move. Even the mill wheels no longer turn, mill wheels which used to collect their harvest of suicides (expectant country lasses who, lacking a father to their children, chose silence in the dank water rather than the horrible susurrus of the village tongues). There was Nancy Webb, for instance, at Passenham Mill. She goes through it once a year with a dreadful shriek, carrying her child in her arms, and her bones crackle in the great wheel like firework squibs. The river makes nothing of this. Ouse by name, say the inhabitants, and ooze by nature. Shake not thy oozy locks at me."

"Gory," said the Countess.

"But oozy is just as good. Those are pearls that were her eyes. Few people realize the beauty of Shakespeare's description. They think of pearls as precious jewels worn by distinguished dowagers at first nights. But they are white stones really, the pale viscous secretion of oysters: a dead, wall-eyed color particularly suitable for the eyes of corpses under the sea. A boiled haddock has much the same look."

"Could we leave Nancy Webb to her grave?"

"Certainly, for she is the least of my ghosts at Passenham. I mention her only because she happens to inhabit the Ouse, and the Ouse is necessary to any description of the village. The mists, you see, come from it.

"Music and mists. The village lies there by the riverside, flat and secluded. It has very few inhabitants now; live inhabitants, I mean, for the dead ones come and go in the mist. Mist into mist, they throng the bridle paths and saunter between the hedgerows. The man who drives the new maids out from Stony Stratford to the big house always says to them, as he drops them at the door, 'I'll be back for you in a month, miss. They never stay longer than that.' Indeed, the only man not frightened of ghosts is old Fowley the sexton. He, when the spirits are more than usually troublesome in November, has been known to walk down the village street brandishing a scythe and exclaiming to the white air: 'I'll larn 'em to come a-plaguing decent people, what have been at the trouble of burying on 'em.' "

"What sort of ghosts do they have in particular at Passenham?"

"Oh, all sorts and conditions. And they find many curious things. The farmer there has a big barn. It's a beautiful thing, ancient, with enormous rafters. They got up to the rafters one day and found a skeleton there, all cramped up, wedged between the beams and the roof. Under the hearthstone in the rectory they dug up two men. Strange doings there must have been, in a strange place, hidden always in the cold mists of the Ouse."

"Murders, I suppose?"

"Oh, yes. Murders and things like that. There were the three louts of Calverton, who slit an old lady's throat for her money, but were caught in Beachampton Grove and hanged behind Calverton Church on a tree. You can still see a carving of them, cut deep outside the church wall."

"It sounds an unfriendly community."

"You might say so. But the ghosts are friendly, of course. Not so much friendly as sociable. They seem to have a liking for company, just as all people do in mists. The fog makes you feel lonely, cut off from your fellow beings, so that when you do see a figure looming up out of the silence it is natural to fall into step beside him. The old sexton would often find somebody walking at his shoulder, but he never paid much heed. He had a kind of acquaintance with them, I suppose, having rumbled the earth down onto most of their coffins. In fact, old Fowley treated them very much like rabbits: a nuisance if they got into the garden and nibbled the vegetables, but nothing more. On the whole the ghosts were respectful toward Fowley. He ignored them in rather a pointed way, and this made them feel inferior. It is galling to be cut by anybody, and to be positively sent to Coventry, as he had done with all the shire ghosts, must have made them feel very small beer. The only time Fowley was ever frightened himself—and then it was more a case of being startled—was on a Sunday night in December. He was verger and general factotum, and he was ringing the church bell for service. He had a lanthorn with him in the belfry, and it blew out, for it was a stormy night. He let go the bell rope to light the lanthorn, and the bell went on ringing. This surprised him, so he took hold of the rope again in the dark: but there was a hand under his own on the rope, a skeleton hand, rather frigid and slippery, and a faint musty smell in the belfry.

"Then there was Robert Bannister, the huntsman. The Whaddon and the Grafton are often over there; sometimes the Bicester. Nobody minds the thunder of the horses' hoofs during the daytime, the earth-shaking music as the cavalry goes by. But it is not nice at night to hear the galloping iron hoofs behind you on a lonely road: possibly just a real horse that has got out of a field by a gate being left open, but possibly not. Would a real horse gallop at midnight, in the pitch dark? And why does it not come nearer? They have put a heavy stone on Bannister in the churchyard to keep him down; but, bless you, as old Fowley says, he doesn't sleep many months together. He rides with his whole pack of hounds in full cry, making a lovely music which sounds more terrible in the darkness, and marks the ground by his grave. He broke his neck out hunting, and was dragged home dead by a frightened horse with his foot in the stirrup. So now he rides like that, a rattling skeleton behind a fiery horse, and the neck is out of joint. It is a fine sight, with the pealing of the hounds and the jolting of the bones, on a roaring northwesterly night of windy December."

"Preserve us!" exclaimed the Countess, putting some more logs on the fire.

"There is a coach, of course, for which the lodge gates open on their rusty hinges, and many another unfortunate wanderer, out of step with time. The place is infested with 'em, in Fowley's phrase; but they won't never hurt ye, man, so long as ye doan't get too much sulphur down your chest as they go by."

"There is a coach over Cheltenham way," said the Countess weakly, "that drives at motorists around one of the bends. People always swerve and go into the ditch; but you don't see it if you put your hat on your knee."

"Indeed," said the Professor. "But I was going to tell you about my concert."

"This conversation," said the Countess, "is making me feel chilly."

"It is the damp," said the Professor.

"Go on, then, if you must."

"I used to know the Vicar of Passenham, a fellow called Brown. Reverent Brown, old Fowley used to call him. He was a stout, hearty fellow that hunted two days a week and preached his sermons out of the *Cambridge Review*. He used to pooh-pooh these ghosts to keep his courage up, and he never let the verger talk about their doings in his presence. A nice fellow in every way, who could generally offer a mount to his friends, and I was in the habit of going down to his vicarage for a day with the Grafton now and then. He put me up one January, a wet, cold month that was more like the fill-dyke of February than the snowy Christmas cards which we are disposed to remember. Even the Ouse had begun to move a bit, it was so full. A misty February, but then it is always fog at Passenham.

"I recollect that Reverent Brown was looking a bit over-wrought when I got down to him, but he said nothing about it, and we had a good day's hunt on Saturday. I made a point of going to church whenever he did—after all, it is only polite when you are staying with a clergyman, and besides, I enjoyed the services in Passenham Church. The oil lamps burned in a kind of halo on the Sunday evening, and the wet fog outside was kept at bay by a primitive heating apparatus that was tended by old Fowley. I liked the bells of Passenham also. They rang out over the water meadows, calling in visitors out of the night. There never was much of a living congregation, but the church did not feel lonely.

"It was a pleasant and unpretentious service, although Brown looked and spoke like a worn man. I read one of the lessons myself, a bit out of an epistle by St. Paul, ill-punctuated as usual. St. Paul never could put a verb into a sentence. I stumbled through it somehow, and the postmistress played 'The Lord's My Shepherd' on the harmonium, and we chanted along after her in the best voice we might. It was music of a sort: better, I suppose, than the silence of the grave."

"Cold," said the Countess.

"Yes," said the Professor. "In the grave it must be very

cold. You could feel all the wet graves about the church, listening as they huddled round it for shelter: the stone graves of the notables, and the headstones cocked sideways to hear better, and the mere grassy oblongs of forgotten toil. It was a well-attended service.

"When Brown had finished he came out of the vestry in his daily clothes and told me to carry off old Fowley to the vicarage for a glass of whisky. It was a raw night, he said, smiling wanly at the old man, for a gentleman to be out in who would never be able to dig his own grave. He himself was feeling like a little music, and would follow us after he had played a couple of hymns. He was tired, he said, and wanted some dull music to settle down. He sat himself at the harmonium as he was speaking; and I went off with the verger, rejoicing in the proximity of a warm drink.

"Fowley's conversation was always original. The vicar, it seemed, had been quite wrong about digging one's own grave. The sexton had dug his own twenty years ago, and trimmed it every Saturday since. This led us naturally to talk of ghosts, and the old fellow told me that they were particularly partial to church bells; would swarm about them, indeed, like bees, during the foggy months. Bells and music, something harmonious to vary the silence of death: anything to pass away the secret tonelessness of earth and stars. Just then we heard the vicar launch out into the 'Dead March' in *Saul*.

" 'Foolhardiness!' remarked old Fowley, shaking his head.

"Ghosts, he told me, had been charmed by the music of Orpheus, who had brought one of them, called Dinah, back from the grave. King Orphew, he added, pronouncing the

160

name in a different way, was a god of the dark himself, as his Greek name testified.

"By this time I was feeling that the conversation had gone far enough. I changed it by remarking that the congregation had been small that night.

" 'We had the usuals,' said Old Fowley.

" 'Do you get bigger gatherings,' I asked, 'at any other season of the year? At harvest festivals, for instance, or Christmas Day?'

" 'The harvest here is a big 'un,' said Fowley, 'and we gets 'em most about All Souls' Day.'

"It was at this point that we heard the vicar wading into the 'Danse Macabre.' Tum-tum, ter-Tum-tum. What on earth could have persuaded him to start that garish and unecclesiastical melody? I remarked wildly to the sexton that Reverent Brown seemed to have an interesting taste in music.

" 'The Nine Tailors,' replied Fowley, 'soothes us all to sleep.'

" 'The present one,' said I, 'is scarcely a soothing tune.'

" 'Perhaps,' said Fowley, 'it is intended for to waken of 'em.'

" 'But the inhabitants of Passenham would scarcely be in bed by now?'

" 'They likes to air their beds.'

" 'What I like,' said I, 'about the country is the feather beds.'

" 'They all likes to sleep soft,' said Mr. Fowley.

" 'Only they are difficult to get out of.'

" 'Difficult to get out of, and difficult to get in. Them that folds their hands to hold flowers, has to have bigger 'uns, for it makes their elbows stick out.'

161

"Reverent Brown was playing Tennyson's funeral hymn. The long moving chords came out of the little church with a strangely quavering intonation. I finished up my whisky.

" 'I was never very good,' said I, 'at getting up in the morning.'

" 'It's music as wakens you best. The curfew bell wakens some on 'em, as the cock-crow puts 'em to sleep, and the music of a trumpet will waken all of 'em on the Last Day.'

" 'That,' added Mr. Fowley, 'is all they have left to 'em. That and the music of the spheres.'

"He left me at this point alone with the whisky bottle, and I could not help pouring myself another stiff tumbler as I waited for the vicar. I was alone in the vicarage, as the maids were out for the evening, and I wandered nervously from one damp room to another: from the moth-eaten antlers in the hall, where a small lamp burned, to the cold beef and pickles laid out for the grace to be said over them in the dining-room. I could not help thinking of the music outside in the reeds of the Ouse, the desolate Pan-piping with which the god of nature used to terrify the ancients, and of all the other ghostly music in the world: the military bands coming back out of the battle, thronged with ghosts, and the pipes in the glen, populating it. At midnight, too, when the dead are supposed to rise, the clocks are playing their longest chimes. All the time the vicar's harmonies kept coming over in shreds from the church porch, and it was getting very late for supper.

"It was an hour before I went over to the church, and the music was still going on. I whistled to keep my spirits up as I crossed the graveyard, but stopped in the middle of a bar as I ran into the sexton. He was sitting on a square tomb looking

up at the windows, which were dark, and remarked on per-
ceiving me: 'Them as whistles at Passenham fetches 'em
round.' I stopped whistling at once.

" 'Is he playing in the dark?' I asked.

"Mr. Fowley nodded to the windows.

"I made an effort, and suggested: 'I think we ought to go
in and fetch him out to his supper.'

" 'Them doors,' said Mr. Fowley, 'is locked.'

" 'Does the vicar usually play in the dark and lock himself
in?'

" 'He hasn't got no keys,' said Mr. Fowley, without turning
his head.

"I need not weary you, as I exhausted myself, with a full
experience of that long winter night. The least I could do was
to stay up outside the church. I sat with old Fowley on the
square gravestone, with the bottle of whisky between us, and
listened to the infernal concert. The sexton talked in snatches
through the fog. King David, he told me, charmed the ghosts
that fluttered around King Saul by playing on his harp: the
Bible prophets summoned their familiars by psaltery, timbrel
and pipe: Elisha sought spirits by making a minstrel play, and
thereby discovered water in the desert: the devil, who was the
greatest of the spirits, doted upon the fiddle, to which he
danced on the witches' sabbath, while the Sanctus bell summoned his opposite angel into church. All the time, as a background to the horrid conversation, we could hear the harmonium plowing its hymns. It exhausted the hymn book
long before dawn, and went off into a ghastly memorization
of the *Students' Song Book*. 'The Londonderry Air' sank to
'Linden Lea,' to the 'Minstrel Boy.' Soon we were in 'The
Vicar of Bray,' 'John Peel,' 'The Bay of Biscay,' 'Down

among the Dead Men' (which was encored), and eventually 'Mademoiselle from Armentières.' Through the whole night the melancholy breathings agonized behind the locked doors, whined for 'Loch Lomond,' jigged with a ghastly bonhomie through Gilbert and Sullivan. It was still dark when the cock crew, and the doors opened to the accompaniment of 'God Save the King.'

"We never saw anything come out. Only, after a bit, there was the vicar in the wet dawn: a drawn and speechless man, peering out of the porch. He never spoke, poor fellow, and is now in Stone asylum. I suppose they must have come to his first notes, come and stood around him in the dark, and made him go on. I dare say he never dared to look over his shoulder, but only went on frozenly with his music. Hair really does stand on end, you know, as you can see if you get yourself sufficiently charged with electricity. When he stopped, the pedals went on moving of their own accord; and the pages were turned over for him. He plays now continually in the asylum. 'Music,' as Mr. Fowley quoted to me when they took him away, 'when soft voices die, vibrates in the memory.' "

The Point of Thirty Miles

"Gentlemen," said Frosty, coughing discreetly, "and ladies, I ought to have said. It is a hunt with the Scurry and Burstall that I am going to describe to you. The strangest hunt and the longest point that ever I was in. Mr. Puffington hunted them in those days, a connection of his late lordship's, in a remote way. His lordship's grandfather married a Jawleyford, and his great-aunt Amelia Jawleyford married a Puffington; so there was hunting in the family. The original Puffington used to hunt the Mangysterne country in the 'fifties; not a very keen master, by all accounts, but an amazing popular man.

"The old Miss Amelia was never really a fox-hunting woman, and nor was old Puffington a born master. Between them they migrated to London and had a large family in the safety of Belgrave Square. The eldest son went into the city and financed sock-suspenders. It was a paying thing, and the Puffington I am speaking of, the grandson, found himself with a convenient house in the Scurry country and a town house in Pont Street. He took after his grandfather and accepted the mastership of the Burstall. My own father sent me to him, as a second whip, when I was a young lad.

"Those were the days for foxes, as my lady and you gentlemen know, before the modern world was pupped; fat sub-

scriptions, stout foxes, fences kept, and nothing to do but
ride all day. It was before the niminy-piminy generation of
motor cars to and from the meet, before the day of horse-
boxes and bath-salts and changed-for-tea at four o'clock.

"It was my last hunt with the Burstall: because my father
was ready to take me back after my apprenticeship, to whip in
for the F.H.H., and because nobody would believe the account which I gave when I got home after it. They seemed to
think that I had been drinking—as, indeed, I had. I was forced
to lie out that night, at a public-house, and after what I'd
been through, drinking seemed to be the reasonable solution.
But I suppose I ought to begin at the beginning. Mr. Puffington was a generous master, mounting his hunt servants in
the very best style, and I had a couple of horses for the meet
at Wingfield Abbey, in their Saturday country. It was a grand
scenting day, a little rain overnight and a cold air to fetch the
smell out of the ground in the morning. The going was good;
not slippery, for the year had been a mild one; and not holding, for it was early in the season and the summer had been
fine. We had a nice dart to begin with; not much of a point,
only a mile and a half, in fact, but a good four as hounds ran,
and we did it in twenty-five minutes. Just at the end of this I
came down at a post and rails. The horse was not really what
I should have called a goer, and I fear that Mr. Puffington
had been done over him. The rails were in a deep bottom,
with a good-sized ditch on the landing side. I saw this ditch
as I was coming up to it, and put on steam as much as I
could. The result was that we hit the top rail, for the horse
was blown and never rose as much as he should have done. I
have no recollection of what happened on the landing side.
Somehow I tore Mr. Puffington's flask off my saddle, which

he used to like me to carry for him, and had to pick it up whilst the others were waiting to come on. I also split my right hand on something, I thought a hoof, and the horse was going awkwardly in the next field. The kennel huntsman held that he had struck himself behind. Fortunately that fox was rolled over within a hundred yards of his point, in another minute, and this gave me time to shake my head and find out where I was. It must have been about twelve o'clock. There was a bit of a palaver, with people casting up and fussing about, and amongst them came my second horse. I hadn't been intended to change over till late, but after I'd told the groom about my rails and moved the horse about in front of him, we decided to make the change at once. I had scarcely got my leg across the second mount, which was a coblike chestnut up to Mr. Puffington's weight, when they were into a second fox out of Yardley's spinneys. They took him quickly back into the spinneys, and out again, having been brought to their noses, on the far side of a rugged fence with an oxer on the one side and wire on the other. We could see across it perfectly, but it would have been lunacy to jump. The hounds came out of the spinney slowly and well together. They were half into the field, almost under the metaphorical shadow of the wire, when a gray creature that looked like a cross between the Benicia Boy and a bear jumped up amongst them. Personally, the first thing I thought of was a sheepdog. There was nothing to be done at all. The Master, who was hunting them because the huntsman had asthma, was on the hither side of the wire with the field, and we whips had cleared off round the spinney. The gray creature just went straight away for a windmill on the skyline, and the hounds went after him, within a few yards, as soon as they had recovered from their surprise. The cry was amazing. The field all turned up the fence and went bucketing along for the nearest gate, which proved to be at the farthest corner of a big enclosure. After that there was no hope of stopping hounds.

"Gentlemen, I must not bore you with the details of the run; and in any case I couldn't, because I have forgotten the country. The important things about it were that our quarry ran practically straight and that I was the only person on a fresh horse. I don't suppose that you have ever hunted a wolf He went away at a tremendous loping pace, a kind of wolf-burst which brought the hounds back to scent within a couple of fields. Then he must have settled to a steadier gait, and he ran like a human being pursued—straight away from his pursuers.

"Like a human being," repeated Frosty meditatively, and the Professor handed him a cigar.

The Countess said: "I thought the last British wolf was killed in the eighteenth century, or something."

"Quite possibly, my lady," replied the huntsman.

"But, my dear fellow," said Mr. Romford plaintively, "either yours was a wolf or it wasn't, and I understand you killed it. You really must make up your mind. It makes a great difference, you know."

"It was difficult," said Frosty-face, "to make up one's mind at all. Our quarry took us ten miles toward the North Sea, running parallel with the Thames, before half-past one. I can't pretend that it was a cracking hunt, not after the first half-hour. The hounds simply ran away from us. When we had properly settled down to it, and after I'd had time to think and realize that the sun was behind my back, I took to the roads with the Master and a few others. After a couple of hours, we merely took the nearest road that seemed to lead eastward and more or less within reported sights of hounds. We went on at these at a goodish pace, but naturally a boring one. There were only five or six in it, and after two hours and a half there was only one objective: to retrieve the hounds somehow or other before dark. Every now and then, but very rarely, we had a bit of country and soft going to make up for the eternal trot and canter along the roads. At four o'clock there was only the Master and myself. He was in a temper and couldn't bring his mount to canter. I offered him mine, but he had worked himself into such a fury about the hounds running riot that he wouldn't listen to anything likely to bring him into salutary touch with them. At the same time I had a faint suspicion that he had by now reached the stage when he preferred his home to his hounds. He simply told me to get along as well as I could, and send him a wire from Dover if I caught them. Well, by now I was excited. Anything like a record is apt to excite a young man. So, although it was not enjoyable, and although my horse was beginning to fade, I set out on my travels with a rising heart. To be the only one up with the hounds on a historic run, perhaps on the most historic run of all! And then there was the nature of the quarry: the last wolf in England. I wondered where on earth it had come from, and wished that it might not prove to be a menagerie creature or a pet. It seemed not to be in the best condition, or else, I suppose, it would have beaten us with ease, but he took us thirty miles. Then, just as it was beginning to get dark, the tide turned in our favor. Scent became burning before it faded, the wolf began to pack up, the tired hounds were drawing up to him, and I established contact with the pack for the first time that afternoon. He was still a good way in front of us, gentlemen, but he was beginning to be a tangible identity. I even winded him myself: a whiff of sour bread and stale bananas. I suppose I ought to have stopped the pack; but he seemed just possible, and I was young. The glory of achievement went to my head."

The huntsman paused to light his cigar with a trembling hand.

"The thing comes back to me very vividly. The love and gratitude which I felt for my broad and striding chestnut; the thrill and fear of the fading quarry and the fading day; the sensation that anything might give at any moment, the horse, the hounds, the wolf or the daylight; the indescribable agony of possibility. Well, everything went; almost within five minutes. First the scent gave out, just as I viewed the wolf. I went mad and lifted the hounds to view, as if I had been doing that sort of thing all my life. And they were as mad as I was, for they rallied to me as if I had always been the Master, and followed where I madly capped them on and shouted. We came to view as the light failed, and the hounds raised a husky cheer just at the moment when my horse gave in. He stood still at a stile which I was trying to put him at, trembled and dropped his head. I left him where he stood, and ran after the hounds like a frantic man, with my spurs biting into my ankles. Then it seemed to get dark almost at a blow, and there was a village with lights in the windows, and a man with a lantern swinging by a barn, and a furious uproar from the hounds, varied by a melancholy cry. I found them by the barn wall, scrumming up against it like a wall-game at Eton College, and two hounds seemed to be dead, and a gray leg was cocked upward above the heaving backs, which drew it to and fro in a terrific worry. The deep-chested savagery of their note was splendid in the lantern-light, terrible, cruel I dare say, but true in kind. They chopped him with an exultant brutality, dragging his entrails, tugging with heads together and heaving shoulders and bloody mouths. But the awful thing, gentlemen, the thing which lost me my place with the Burstall when I reported it, was that the wolf was trying to articulate. Against the background of their full-blooded ferocity there was a thin and guttural note, a human supplication, an enunciation on the borders of the English tongue. The werewolf's leg, gentlemen, that was cocked above the scrummage, turned pink, grew hairless, convulsed itself like a kicking frog's: and Challenger was trotting around the outside of the circus, with a hand of human fingers in his mouth."

The Professor said, in a hushed voice: "Well, Frosty, you take the biscuit."

The huntsman touched his forehead with a pleased smile.

"It isn't," continued the Professor, "that I don't know how to loose the arrow a little on the far side myself. I could have told you quite a good story about the Hunt Cup at Cheltenham, in which Mr. Siegfried Sassoon ran a horse called Pegasus, that was disqualified because it was found to have wings. But, after a werewolf, what's the use?"

A Rosy Future, Anonymous

She was within six weeks of her twentieth birthday. She was Irish, a Catholic and therefore a virgin. She was pretty in an uncertain, grubby, hopeful way. Her hair was done in the fashion of last year's films, and her cheap dress was of the same date: not because she had no eye for the mode, but because she could not afford to buy clothes often. She had been a typist in Dublin, but she had saved up seven pound ten, as well as the money for her ticket, so that she could run away from home. She had never been in an airplane before, and the name on her ticket was not her own. She was going to London to seek her fortune. Her name was Moira.

The pilot sent back a notice for the passengers, saying that they were at seven thousand feet, and would reach the airport at about six o'clock. They looked out of the windows at the vibrating, studded wings: at the crackled sea crawling beneath them. It was an opal, winter evening, with no horizon. The dove-colored haze and the flamingo cumulus clouds at their own level joined with the frosty ocean, without a line between. The passengers pondered, without being able to express themselves, upon the levels of life. Their air-fish floated in the lofty shade, as the sea-fish floated far below them, while, on the surface, a toad of a tug forged steadily along, trailing its legs for wake. All were in the aquarium. The regular herringbone pattern of the waves did not fit with the surf or the whitecaps. That is to say, there were no regular lines of foam, as there would be on a beach. Instead, the sea-flowers disclosed themselves irregularly, scattered here and there over the neat remote corrugation. Surf? Scurf? It was like dandruff on the flat, gray coat of sea, seven thousand feet below the determined wing.

There were only five other passsengers. One of them was known to Moira: he was a Dublin bookie. Two others were evidently a honeymoon couple: the girl nervous, picking at her gloves, the man stiff in a new suit with buttonhole flower and his flat hat brim tilted at the correct gangster angle, both self-conscious. In public, the Irish are a silent race. There was a nun, a Benedictine, calmly tucked away in the mercy of God. There was a distinguished man in English clothes and black homburg hat, carrying a briefcase, gray hair at his temples, like Anthony Eden. Moira thought he must be a diplomat.

And when we land at London Airport, thought the maiden, perhaps he will leave the briefcase on his seat, forgetting it. I will pick it up, with an unhurried, dainty movement, and follow him gracefully to the Customs barrier. There, as he waits for his smart suitcases to be examined (pigskin), I will say to him in a cool, thrilling voice—a real woman of the world—I will say: "Excusing me, aye believe you have mislaid this article?" And he will say: "My dear lady! Thank Heaven you have found it in time! In that briefcase lie the secret articles of a treaty between Sir Winster Churchill and Misther De Valera, which, had they have had been lost, well might there have been a conflergation between ould England and the twenty-six Counties! You are the Savior of our race!"

"Don't mention it," I will say distantly, giving him to understand that I am not one of thim trotties . . . No, the story
was going wrong. "You're welcome," I will say. "Sure, it was
just under me hand." "A pretty hand," Mr. Eden will say, "the
milk-white hand of a true Irish colleen! Madam, allow me to
express the thanks of Her Majesty's Government with per-
found respec." And then, for all diplomats do, he will raise
me fingers to his lips—I must wipe them (she did so, on her
skirt: they were pink, innocent fingers)—and, as his gray
moustache just brushes the inds of me knuckles, he will mur-
mur: "My Princess!"

Or perhaps there would be one of the Rolls Royces waiting, a long, black car with initials in front instead of a badge,
and he would say: "Allow me to drop you at your luxurious
flat in—in Buckingham Palace?" No. It had to be *possible*. She
had no flat: she could not be dropped anywhere. She did not
want the rosy dream to become a fantasy. It had to be practical, within the bounds of possibility.

Perhaps he would insist on taking her to Downing Street,
to be thanked in person by the Prime Minister. But she did
not particularly want to meet Sir Winster, who was far too
old and married in any case. Come to think of it, so was Mr.
Eden married. Perhaps the diplomat would be some kind of a
bachelor duke, for there were many such in the Diplomatic,
and he would take her to see his mother the countess, for
Afternoon Tea.

Her little finger crooked in her lap, as she thought of
this.

When they were married, she would be a duchess herself.
He would have to change his religion, of course, for love of
her, unless he happened to be one of the Catholic dukes, like

the Duke of Norfolk, who unfortunately was also married. And she would live in a great house like the Duke of Leinster's, with a silver cream jug and perfume by Guerlain and clothes of sheer nylon underneath-like, nothing immodest, and she would go sometimes in the Rolls Royce to visit her ould Da—she would give him one as well, or perhaps ever such a nice cottage at Bray with an electric blanket—and she would buy Father Flood that picture he wanted and pay back the nine shillings she borrowed from Esther McMennamin. She would pay it back in a letter on pink paper with a crown on it, and oh, how impressed Esther would be, when a dimond broach also fell out of the letter as a token of gratitude!

Then, when they had some babies who would be knights— Sir Patrick, Sir Eugene and Sir Desmond—she would grow old gracefully in Buckingham Square, or whatever the best square in London was called, and be at all the charity concerts in a tara. Her husband the duke would say to her: "My dear, sure it was the turning point of me life, alannah, that moment when I met ye in the airyplane from Dublin, and it's a happy man ye've made me this many years, God be praised for it."

Moira was not avaricious or selfish. She was determined to make the duke happy in return for the happiness he was going to give her, and she knew quite well that the whole world had not been made for her own enjoyment only. She meant to be a true wife to her duke and a loving mother to her children. All the same, she wanted to have the nylons.

Meanwhile, the humming wing bored steadfastly into the twilight, over the skirted coast, over a golf course. The bunkers of the course were exactly like the impressions of a

thumbnail. For some reason it had been bombed in the last
war and the scars were clearly visible from the air, small moon
craters of dead tissue on the vast, darkling, homely, patterned,
populated flesh of England. The motor cars, miniature crawling beetles on the maplike roads, were switching on their side
lights. Outside Moira's window the mysteries of lift and drag
flowed mightily about the airfoil, on which pieces of cotton,
had they been tied, would have stood upright.

They would be there soon. She must dismiss her diplomat.
There was an airport bus, she knew, which would take her to
a place in Kensington, and there another bus of a certain
number—she looked it up in her letter—would convey her to
Mrs. Pilkington's, as nursery governess. She must dismiss the
diplomat for now: he would be for the future. Inconstant
maid, ruthlessly feminine, she switched him off. But why
need he have been so absolutely impossible? A kitten of nearly twenty, surely she might be forgiven for making some
small paw-pats of the imagination?

Over London, in the darkness, the myriad streets swung
like the spokes of a wheel, all lighted. The window lights, the
whole unending hive, twinkled. This was because each fore-
ground chimney passed across each background window, as
the airplane bee-hived past, making a flicker of intercep-
tions.

The stewardess delivered a message at each of the seats.

"We shall be ten minutes before we land, as we have been
told to orbit."

And she would be famous! There was time to go on thinking a little about the duke. Not just a typist, not a governess,
but the great, the distinguished and beautiful Duchess of
Wales! She would do good, too, and give money to the poor

and found a convent and perhaps discover something, like
Madam Cury on the filum. There would be a moniment for
her when she was dead, and many, many masses said for her
soul. The duke's too. And the childern's.

The Duchess of Wales!

The door at the front opened, under the notice which
could be lighted up to forbid smoking, and a man with a very
red face came into the cabin. He was one of those who blush
with fear, instead of paling. But he was collected.

He said: "Will you do up your straps, please? We are going
to make an emergency landing."

The stewardess, who was one of those who went white
instead of red, came from the back seat, bearing barley sugar.
Routine gives people something to do. She said that there
was no cause for alarm. The red-lit notice said "NO SMOK-
ING." There seemed to be a smell of petrol.

Nobody had time to begin a rosary, or anything in the
dramatic tradition. Outside her starboard window, Moira saw
a very quick trickle of fire curvetting along the carrot-shaped
cowling of the engine in drops, and this, in a brief moment,
before her heart could plunge, stretched out astern in a yard-
wide shaving-brush or blowlamp of strontium-colored
flames. While her mouth was still opening, the cabin tilted
away to port, so that she clutched the arm of her seat, then
the handbag on her lap, and bumped her forehead on the
window. The rosy blowlamp pointed away from her along
the wing. Then there was one great puff of blazing yellow,
like the time when the paraffin lamp blew up at her Da's and
singed off her eyebrows: but she had no time to think of
that.

A Rosy Future, Anonymous

*　*　*

The morning papers reported that there were no survivors.
They gave the names of the crew. The passengers were:
  Mr. Eamon McCowen, 53, bookmaker, Dublin.
  Mr. and Mrs. Ryan, Connemara.
  Sister Ursula Mary, Kylemore.
  Mr. J. Smith, 47, commercial traveler, Ealing.

One body had not been identified.

Not Until Tomorrow

The boy lay face downward in the tremendous forest, adoring. He was unusually beautiful, like most of the Plantagenets were. His grandfather was said to have had a face like a god's, his great-great-grandfather was supposed to have been the strongest man in the kingdom—much as King George the Fifth was supposed to be the best shot—and his mother was known by the common people as the Fair Maid of Kent. He had yellow hair, at that age, and the carved lips of a pocket Rameses in granite. Like all charming faces, it was already inclined to be sad or brooding, as if beauty were its own tragedy, which perhaps it is. He was only ten years old.

Diccon was adoring the forest: the sun-eggs which dappled the sward (it was July), the humming horn of insects in numbers astronomical, the birdsong still rising and ringing through the leaves, and particularly a number of flies which had decided to sit on the underside of every leaf within sight, so that, as the filtered sun shone through the leaves from the other side, each leaf became a transparent green bun with one currant in it.

Nearly six hundred years have passed since the boy lay in the greenwood, brimming with life. They are years which have altered the forest, so that perhaps only a few of his acorns remain as our oldest oaks, and which have altered the face of his countryside beyond recognition. Indeed, the glade where he lay is somewhere under the pavements of Croydon. If we want to go back to him and to understand, we shall have to disremember forty million Cockneys hating each other's pasty faces in tunnels under the earth; we shall have to forget the smokestacks and the clang and the advertisements for Aspro and the expensive weapons of destruction. In his day there were only two or three million backwoodsmen in all the treeful counties of England; there were treetrunks for factory chimneys, the little witchcrafts of old wives instead of Aspro, the long bow of Wales instead of the Spitfire, and a blessed silence in the towns. But above all, if we are to beat down the difference between us, we must be able to imagine the forest itself, which he was worshipping.

It was enormous. Half of England was a wood. Think of the touching branches from Portsmouth to Peterborough, and the billion leaves in their silence or song, and the ashy trunks rising by one and one, in colonnades, garrisons, army corps, empires. Think of the winter winds which whined through their skeletons in the Old England, and of the west winds in spring and autumn which roared through their foliage and tossed their uncountable arms till the roof of the forest heaved like porridge. Think of them in snow, holding up the heavy drapery like bushes over which the housewife spreads her washing; think of them in the tender green of May, drenched with the parachute notes of the woodlark. Think how full they must have been of life: full of the red squirrels which we shall soon see no more, skipping from bole to bole in a shower of twigs and curses: full of pigeons and pheasants, big squabs in gold mail, which were tamer than ours because they had never been fired at: full of creepers and crawlers beyond counting. The herons preened themselves in their untidy nests, greeting their mates with hoarse cries like the road-drill's, kak-kak-kak-kak-kak. Even goshawks were there, in freedom, not to mention the wolves and the deer which the kings loved like their own children and the wild boars, now gone. Much of what was not forest was fen. There, in the flat immensities around the Wash and the Humber, the bitterns boomed and the harriers swept their shadows over the reeds, while the wildfowl quacked or whistled and a seashore younger by five centuries than ours was shrill with piping.

Nor is it safe to idealize the enormous forest, for in some ways it was jungle. There, as Diccon's favorite poet said, one could part the bushes and find oneself face to face with a cold corpse sitting upright, open-mouthed. There was the smyler with the knife under his cloak, there the cadaver in the thicket with its throat cut. The trees were the perfect underworld. You raised your hand in anger, had a sudden difference with the tax collector: just for a moment the red rage blazed and the sharp edge jarred on the bone. Then you stepped over the body and opened the back door, and there was the greenwood waiting for you: half of England. It was a hard life, not a matter of camping in a game preserve. You would have to sleep, in wind or sleet, under some tangled root or overhanging bank or hasty booth of branches, with the wild animals, in the jungle. There were regular bands of your fellows, cutthroats without a moral between them, but often with that sardonic humor which amoral people seem to have. They named their gangs poetically, sometimes, saying they were the Men of King Arthur, or of Robin Hood, or the Minions of the Moon. Some of them were on their keeping for respectable reasons, not for homicide. It was only three hundred slow years since the bastard had invaded. Then, at the invasion, his Normans had butchered and dispossessed the real inhabitants like Huns in Poland. The pursuit of the dispossessed was still dragging on vaguely at the edges of the last strongholds—in wild Wales and further Scotland and among the mere Irish. Several of these kind of people, still dedicated to the ancient and absolutely irretrievable sovereignty of Saxon or Celt, lived in the forest or the fen, free. They had secret societies. Their outlaws' heads were the wolf's head, and they were to be killed like wolves.

Above all, there were the socialists and communists, demagogues or ideologists or louts. Twenty years before Diccon was born, Europe had been devastated by the most ghastly plague in history. Before it came, there had been four million people in England: after it had stopped, there had been about two and a half. Nearly half the people in the known world had died, all in one year. The effect on the labor market had been terrible. It was the opposite of "unemployment:" there had been too much employment, which was possibly worse. The laboring man suddenly, in one year, had doubled his value, and the employer had halved his profits.

So the forest was full of communists who went about saying that the church was humbug, particularly the rich friars, and the monarchy and the nobles were thieves who had stolen the means of production from the proletariat. "When Adam delved and Eve span," they said, like a conundrum, "who was then the Gentleman?" One of their leaders preached in a sermon: "The matters gothe nat well to pass in Englonde, nor shall not do till every thinge be commune."

184

Also, we had been at war with France for forty years, a war of pillage.

Old soldiers whose trade was killing: labor leaders: racial agitators: homicides: wont-works: assassins: professional thieves: perhaps some few innocent men who really loved freedom, just as there were very many who said they did: all these made up the men of the forest, who took their secret way about in it along private runways, like the rabbit's, but with keen steel handy.

"For an outlaw," said the stay-at-homes:

"For an outlaw, this is the law,
That men him take and binde,
Without pitee, hanged to be,
And waver with the winde."

In Diccon's day, it was easy to be an outlaw. There were four main classes of people: the nobility, the clergy, the town-ees and the country laborers. These last were the representatives of the earlier races which the Normans had chased away or taken prisoner. They were more or less without rights, except for the power of custom and corporate action, and in theory they belonged to the first two classes, like cattle. But in practice they were not without freedom. Often they had thirty acres arable of their own, and, since the Black Death, their bargaining power had doubled itself. The upper classes naturally legislated against them, saying that they must not strike for higher wages or for more freedom, and that they must not leave the farms they were born on, in search of a better life elsewhere. Those of them who had a defined sense of justice, or who were stiff-necked, or who only were sturdy and lazy and preferred to be vagabonds, did run away from their masters all the same, and many became outlaws.

There was something American about the forest, both North and South American. The little villages in the clearings were like settlements of Canadian lumberjacks: through and about these filtered the counterparts of the Negro slave, escaping from the south: and everywhere there was the cattle-lifting and the posse and the galloping sheriff who has come to be associated with the Wild West, all mixed together in the mystery of the woodland, which might have banked the Amazon. Also, in the towns, there was already a kind of Chicago atmosphere, and the Lords Mayor went with body-guards at elections.

These things were part of what Diccon was adoring. They say that children are barbarians, and for Diccon all the bloodshed and arrowing and wavering ragbound in the wind were part of a glory, a game of Red Indians in real life. He had armed men about him, within call, and it was safe for him to lie there on his face, misinterpreting the world.

For he did misinterpret it. He was too kind-hearted, loving and fond of beautiful things. Although he enjoyed the idea of the wild wood and of the bandits and of the noble clash of armor, although he even enjoyed the idea of the outlaw on his gibbet so long as that outlaw was a kind of wicked uncle justly throttled for his outrages, when he met a real one, some wretched Hawkyn, Dawkyn, Tymkyn or Tyrry, begging for alms with mormal on shin, Diccon wept if he were not allowed to give the fellow money. One of the standing jokes against him was that he had cried on first learning the nature of a sardine! He had been eating the thing, in Bordeaux, when he was four years old, and he had asked his Nannie what it was. When old Mundina told him that it was a dead fish with its head cut off, he had burst into tears. He knew what a live fish looked like. But fancy crying about a fish, said his cousin Harry contemptuously! Knowing about the sardine was one of Harry's holds over him.

Thinking of Harry, whom he disliked, made Diccon think of his Uncle Thomas, whom he disliked more. His uncle was twelve years older than himself, that is he was twenty-two. It was the age to intimidate a boy of ten, not old enough to be safely classed as "old," but enough to be unpleasantly superior and different and physically intimidating. Uncle Thomas and his bosom friend the Earl of Arundel were horrible. It is difficult to explain, but they were rank. Their wenching and male selfishness and successfulness with their bodies in hunting and war and tournaments and in the athletic things, and their purposely blunt minds, and their contempt because he loved colors or music, and the sandy pig's bristles on their forearms, these things went against his fur. He was uncomfortable before them, like a dog with a cat. They humiliated him with the arrogant secret of gender. They looked at him.

He would not think about them.

Diccon turned over on his back, and peered up the tree-boles from underneath. They went up like spars into the greenery, and the shafts of sunlight which came through to make the sun-eggs picked out all sorts of tiny insects, in theatrical spotlights. Eight feet above his nose, there was a small spider playing itself out at the end of a single thread, and thread and spider burned in a minute splendor of gold.

It was glorious to be alive, glorious to be Diccon. I! Me! I will do this: I will do that: I will be glorious as the world is glorious, and I will ride its beauty at my will. If it were possible to see boy and man together, the same person with forty years of life between them: to hear the clear soprano challenge and the anesthetized bass at the same moment, perhaps few would survive it.

Meanwhile, it was still the glory of the beginning. He would be the greatest king in Christendom, and he would settle all these villeins so that everybody was happy, and he would wear a surcoat made entirely of gold cloth, a tight-fitting one, and he would have his old Burley turned into a duke, and he would give his Nannie a pension, twice as much as anybody ever had, and he would get a gyrfalcon for Robert de Vere, and he would buy his mother the biggest crown in the world, simply covered with the biggest jewels, so that she would not be sad any longer because his father was dead.

But the thought made him miserable. He had remembered his father. The heavy, swollen, sick, humorless man was before him, kind and looming and dying of dropsy. Later ages have for some reason come to call him the Black Prince, but nobody ever called him that while he was alive. They called him Old Lead Foot. He had been a silent father, who watched one playing without comment: a formidable person to some people, but Diccon had pitied and adored him. He had been the greatest soldier there ever was. He had won the battles of Crécy and Poitiers (against odds of ten to one) and he had captured the King of France himself, alive-o! His motto, apart from Ich Dien, had been "Houmout"—which meant, more or less, "guts." Diccon did not know it, but his marriage with the Fair Maid of Kent had been a runaway match, when neither of the parties had been chickens. Lead Foot had been thirty-one and his wife thirty-three, a widow with three children of her own, when he married her for love, without the old king's consent. And then there had been a few years of love with honor, and then the dysentery and the dropsy, and some people said poison. It was the poisoned hulk that Diccon had pitied, appreciating with childhood's acute eye the tragic contrast between the end and the beginning. At last there had been the week when he had not been allowed to see his father, and after that there had been the canon and the huge candles and the still, blueish face, badly shaved, looking solemn as if it knew something and more leaden than ever.

Where was his father, the suffering man who had been a great conqueror? Was he under the ground? Could he see you? They said that this awful thing came for everybody, and would come eventually even for him, even for Diccon.

But it was a long way off: there was infinite time before him, and he need not think about it. Perhaps he would live to be a hundred, and then go to heaven in a chariot, like the man in the sermon.

Or perhaps he would die tomorrow. On the very steps of the throne, he would falter, turn deadly pale, and clutch his heart—like this. "No, mother," he would say, as she rushed up to catch his falling body, "it is too late. I die for England!" And then Uncle Thomas would be sorry he had been beastly. And everybody would cry, and say what a wonderful person he had been, and he would have a tremendous funeral, and the whole land would mourn . . .

He got tired of the funeral, and turned his head sideways, to look along the ground. The bracken and small bushes and saplings made a miniature forest of their own, under the roof-tree of the real forest. They had their own small glades and dangerous places, with fierce tiny animals (insects) ready to rush out from ambush in their outlaws' webs. If I were as small as a spider, he thought, these bits of bracken would be trees to me, and the real trees would be kind of mountains. How strange it would be if there were enormous trees in the world, as much bigger than these real trees as these real trees are bigger than the bracken. Yes, and if there were smaller weeds under the bracken, to which the bracken would be like real trees. Then everything would fit into everything else, so that every small thing had the same thing above it bigger, and the same thing under it smaller, and all the worlds would fit inside other worlds, until finally what?

He looked up, and there was Harry watching out of a bush.

"What on earth are you doing?"

"I was thinking."

"Why?"

Harry never thought about anything except saddles and armor and keeping his heels down when he was riding and about who was top of the tilting averages. How could you tell him that you were thinking about being as small as a spider? Diccon felt ashamed at the very thought, and began to lie desperately. You had to tell Harry that you had been thinking about something to do with the done things, and he hastily made something up.

"I was thinking," he said, grandly, "of augmenting my own arms, because I am the font of honor."

"Oh."

"I shall super-charge a gold cross on a silver shield."

"Why?"

"Because it will be beautiful."

"It may be beautiful," said Harry, "but it will be metal on metal."

And he began to laugh contemptuously. He had got his cousin where he wanted him. In heraldry it was practically an absolute rule that metals could never be put on metals nor colors on colors, just as nobody puts the two slices of bread together in a sandwich. The unlucky gold cross ought to have been on a colored shield, or, if he had wanted a silver shield, the cross ought to have been colored. Putting metal on metal was as bad as dropping H's. Diccon began to blush.

"It would be beautiful, all the same."

And, of course, it would have been.

"Beautiful!" said Harry. "Pretty, pretty, pretty!"

"The King of Jerusalem bears gold crosses on silver."

"That's because Jerusalem is different from anywhere else, and is in the center of the world, and it's done on purpose."

"Well, I'll be different from everybody else."

"But you're not."

"I . . . "

It was no good. Harry had a way of not looking in a person's eyes, except when he knew he could stare you out, and, as this habit is catching to sensitive people, it was impossible to look in his.

"Anyway," said Harry, "it's no good moping about here. Everybody is bating in all directions looking for you, and Burley is having a fit, and your Nannie has come from the castle, and it's your bedtime."

He raised his voice and shouted: "Hullo, everybody, hullo! Here he is. I've found him. He's in the glade."

So he had spoiled that too. He had been hiding on purpose, because he knew that the son of the King of France had once been lost for several days in a forest, by himself, and there had been a fuss about it. He had wanted to enjoy a fuss about himself, though of course he would have come back grinning before it got serious. Now he was to be hauled off ignominiously by Harry, and the whole thing was a flop. What made it unbearable was the stuff about bedtime. Harry was the same age as himself, and the old king had knighted them on the same day, but Harry said he had not got a bedtime and always made it plain that he thought Diccon a ninny for having one. Harry rode horses superbly (everyone said so) and was exact about heraldry and had drank some whisky and was a superior person, and he knew that poor Diccon was a sham.

Everybody began to arrive, puffing.

Sir Simon Burley was in the first wave, looking more mulberry-colored than ever. He was flustered, and was just going to say H'm, in order to express himself. He had a good deal to express. In the first place, he had really thought that his pupil was lost, and in the second place he had just been insulted by Mundina because it was past the boy's bedtime. With these long summer days, and the, h'm, sun still shining busily, and, h'm, and . . .

"H'm," said Sir Simon.

Mundina, who was in the second wave, said: "Now then, Master Diccon, it's time little boys was in bed, and you leading us such a dance, though how some people can have the heart to leave the precious little mite meandering through the purlieus unbeknownst, for so it was, as I say, though it should be denied a thousand times, is more than some people would care to mention, not if it was ever so."

"I don't want to go to bed."

"Little heads . . . "

It was frightful. Did women do this maliciously, on purpose to humiliate the male, or were they devoid of feeling? Little heads and little boys and little mites, in front of Harry, in front of everybody!

"I don't want to go to bed," he shouted, "and I won't go to bed!"

"Indeed you will, and that this minute."

"I won't, won't, won't, won't, won't!"

"Come along now, Master Diccon, or you'll be smacked."

Smacked!

The last twist of the knife.

"I won't go to bed," he said. "I won't go home. I hate you. I hate you. How dare you speak to me like that? I am the King of England."

"Oh, no, you're not," said Mundina promptly, "not until tomorrow."

And she collared him with an experienced hand. The horses were brought at once, the picnic was over, and they all rode off to Westminster.

On the way home, Diccon thought bitterly: What is the good of being ten? Even if I am crowned tomorrow, it will be ages and ages before I am allowed to do anything. There will be masses of uncles and councils of regency and nannies and tutors and can't do this and can't do that and wait till you are a big boy.

It seemed a terrible time before he could ever be the King of England.

The Philistine Cursed David by His Gods

"My father's grandfather on his mother's side," said Mary, "was a Yorkshire squire of the name of Hance. He was born to a generous inheritance on the distaff side, and was the eldest of four brothers; but he was only twenty-seven inches high."

"Is this," asked the Professor, "going to be a crib on Huxley?"

"Not entirely," said Mary. "The problem is different. In fact it is the kind of problem that demands a title, and I shall call it, 'The Philistine Cursed David by his Gods.' You will be able to guess the dilemma as we go along."

"Loike a bleeding parlor game," said Facey to Soapey behind his hand, thinking of the Nap which nobody would play. Miss Springwheat ignored the interruption.

"My great-grandfather flourished in the early nineteenth century, in the time of Osbaldeston, and Coke of Norfolk, and Lord George Bentinck. In order to understand his story you will want a knowledge of his period, and so you must forgive me if I begin to get a bit historical.

"The early nineteenth century is a period which fascinates me more than others. There has never been a mode for it, because it was too short and peculiar to leave a cult. Elizabethanism and Georgianism and Victorianism have all been taken up by fashionable people with cultural pretense, but nobody has ever invented an enthusiasm for the afterglow of William the Fourth. It is because the period was brief. It was transitional, individual, complicated, but with an amazing bouquet. It smelled dimly of the Regency, dimly of mahogany, but more than anything else of country life.

"I don't know how to explain it, or which peculiarities to collect. You must think of shooting and hunting and boxing and betting and left-handed alliances and port.

"I think the betting, really, is the important trait. Everybody betted about everything, and nearly everybody was ruined. Why did people bet? Well, I suppose to a certain extent they did so to escape from tedium. Prinny, for instance, betted about the flies on the rainy window pane because there was nothing else to do. The means of transport were so slow, one was so much of a fixture in whatever place one happened to be in, that a selection of parlor games were needed, and places to play them. One betted at the clubs. The Anglesey Stakes at Goodwood defined a Gentleman Rider as a member of White's, Brooke's, Boodle's, or one of six other fraternities. It was a simple definition, but it met the case. Everybody who was a gentleman belonged to a club, and in the club he lost his money.

"The main cause behind the wagers was something other than tedium. It was a peculiar phobia, very distinctive of the period. It was a matter of courage.

"When Henry Mytton jumped the park railing or locked his wife in the kennels, or hunted with a broken arm, he was producing an attitude toward courage. He was showing or encouraging bravery and endurance with a fanatical zeal. Endurance for him was the important thing in the world. Perhaps it was because the people of the eighteenth century had so much to endure. Think of the Loblolly man, who held you down for amputation without anesthetics in naval engagements, and the cockfights, and the pugilists, and the schoolboys killing each other at Eton, and the birch of Dr. Keate. Ferocity, Courage, Endurance. It was the craze of the century. Osbaldeston betted that he would ride two hundred miles in ten hours, and he did it in less than nine. That is the perfect example, which made him the first man in the country. The nation rose to him and called him the Squire of England. It was because he showed endurance; and financial courage beside it, in the money match.

"You see, people wagered for courage. They wanted to show that they were not afraid to lose. They wanted to be brave in every way, even against the forces of hazard. England was a second Sparta. Henry Mytton burned himself to death to show that he could bear physical pain; Osbaldeston, after being jumped on by Sir James Musgrave, lying on the ground with his boot full of blood and the bones protruding through the skin, remarked, "I am so unlucky that I *think* I shall give up hunting," and did not; a member of the Portland Club played billiards for twenty-four hours on end; a man called Baker walked sixty-five miles in one day, and two thousand miles in forty-two; a Mr. T. of Kensington bet 150 guineas that he would drive his tandem full speed against the wheels of the first seven vehicles he should meet on the Brentford Road, and won in twenty-five minutes.

"Imagine a motorist of the present day offering to drive his car against the wheels of the first seven lorries on the Great

North Road. It seems to be lunacy. And yet it is the kind of lunacy that makes an appeal, if you understand it. It was the lunacy of endurance and courage; and it was the lunacy of something besides. These lunatics were individuals. Perhaps that is the most important glimpse of all.

"A gentleman in the first half of the nineteenth century was a person who existed by himself. He lived quite obviously in his own world and was ultimately alone in it. This is true of a person in any century, but it took an early Victorian to realize the truth. Once the fact was realized a certain attitude of mind developed naturally. Osbaldeston knew that he was alone, knew that in the last resort the only thing he truly possessed was his own sturdy little body. He had acres and houses and clothes to dress the body in, but finally speaking these were only trappings. He was a nude male of little over five feet, weighing eleven stone. That was his weapon in a hostile and frequently painful world. Painful in the literal sense: think of the lack of anesthetics, the country dentist, and the activities of Dr. Keate.

"Well, the one weapon was bound to react. It had to meet the hostilities and the pain. It had to be capable of vanquishing them in its own person, stripped of the acres and the clothes. That was why the nobility learned to box, why pugilism was a noble art. Physically, individually, as a special, single and metaphorically naked man, the gentleman of the early nineteenth century pitted himself against the universe and backed himself to win. You had to bet on yourself; you had to be able to stand on your own legs and carry money on them. The wager was an affirmation of your personality, a defiance of the surrounding world, a challenge issued against the flogging authorities and the malevolent gods. Mr. T. of

Kensington was a man who was not afraid of destiny. He believed in himself. His spartan prowess, his physical courage and power to endure, were at bottom a defense of the individual.

"And what individuals they were! James Hirst of Rawcliffe used to hunt with the Badsworth on a bull, and had trained a black sow to stand game. She was excellent with partridge, pheasant, blackgame, snipe and rabbit, but never pointed a hare. A certain Mr. Ireland bet a certain Mr. Jones that he could cover one hundred yards in fewer than thirty hops, and did it in twenty-one. It scarcely comes as a surprise that the Rev. Robert Lowe, the sporting parson of Nottinghamshire, should have had two daughters with red eyes and white hair, who could only see in the dark.

"Well, I have said all I can do about the period, without feeling successful, and at the risk of being dull. Perhaps I ought to say something about the atmosphere. Have you ever for several days on end got up at half-past five for cubbing and at half-past four to shoot the early season duck? You remember the appetite for breakfast, and the mixed feeling of the afternoon, conscious of tingling eyelids and hardy muscles, and the drugged sleep at night. It is the healthy endurance of the eighteenth century. Those were the sports which these people indulged in. The Regency atmosphere, in which the betting was nocturnal and urban, had given place to a country air. The feats of Osbaldeston were feats on horseback and with guns. The early Victorian rose early and affirmed his singular manhood before dawn. The Squire of England hunted six days a week, staying in the saddle eleven hours a day, and kept his bed till noon on Sunday for a change.

"It was in this atmosphere that my great-grandfather Hance was saddled with the necessity of supporting his twenty-seven inches. You see that it was needful to define the atmosphere in order to explain his problem. He was twenty-seven inches high, in a world where it was necessary to be an individual, and a physically conquering one at that. Men, like horses, had to endure and to achieve. The unhappy Rattler, an American trotter, trotted thirty-six miles at sixteen or seventeen miles an hour, and died of it. Naturally it was for a bet.

"My great-grandfather Hance was a sporting gentleman with the best, a gentleman of the Fancy. They called him Little Tommy, and he came in for a good deal of chaff during the ascendancy of Jackson's famous Tom Thumb. You might have thought that his stature would have assured him of his admission as an individual amongst those individual bucks. Perhaps it might have done, but Little Tommy was not contented with a success of esteem which depended upon his peculiarity alone. He was horribly sensitive, doomed by his destiny to make good.

"Moving in a world of giants who asserted themselves by muscle, of masters of hounds who fought their post-boys with bare fists and controlled their fields by setting about them with a hunting crop, the dwarf found himself oppressed by physique. Everything that made for greatness seemed so terribly physical, so overbearingly measurable in beef and bone. Perhaps he might have retired from the contest, making himself his own intellectual world like Pope or Voltaire. But Little Tommy was sharpened by the challenge, and went out to meet the Philistines on their own ground.

"He used to hunt with Sir Richard Sutton's hounds, on a

mount that was less than fifteen hands but still seemed ridiculously big for him. Nobody could cut him down. Even in those days, when Fernely could paint a scene near Melton that depicted a fox in front, then a member of the field, then several more members braining a solitary hound, then the main body, then the master blowing his horn, and then the hounds running in the opposite direction: even in those days of green-eyed jealousy, nobody could cut Little Tommy down. He rode in the first flight, with Sir James Musgrave and Assheton Smith. He had trained himself to be able to drink a bottle of port without reeling, which was by no means bad for his capacity, and he shot with precision, using a toy gun whose bore might have corresponded to our own fourten. He was a great man for the then new-fangled introduction of the percussion cartridge.

"My great-grandfather owned an estate in Yorkshire, of about fifteen thousand acres, and it was there that he used to entertain the famous shots. Shooting in the eighteen-twenties was curiously different from the shooting now. On the one hand the weapons were primitive, on the other the game was easy. The sportsman had to discharge a heavy flintlock, tediously loaded, which hung fire between the pulling of the trigger and the issue of the shot. A double-barrel was considered unsporting. In spite of this cumbersome and inaccurate contrivance, the famous marksmen were able to record amazing feats: one hundred pheasants with one hundred shots, ninety-seven consecutive grouse, and twenty brace of partridges with forty shots from an eighteen-bore. Their prowess was accounted for by the nature of the game. Crops then were cut by hand, so that the stubble stood high and birds could be walked up close. The birds themselves were less wild. The guns were sometimes of an astonishing caliber. Osbaldeston was in the habit of shooting pigeons with a bore whose diameter was an inch and a half.

"Little Tommy used to entertain his guests at Bushel, and reveled in the entertainment. His shooting was magnificent, so that the guest was pleased to be polite in return for the sport, and the dwarf used to be able to sun himself in the equality which his muscular giants seemed to offer. He had a charming wife, whose mother had been the penniless widow of a dean, and he could boast of her beauty without fear or favor throughout the county. The only immediate cross he had to bear was the neighborhood of Sir Marcus Izall, the landlord of an extensive property which marched with his own.

"Sir Marcus Izall came of a family older than the Squire's. There seemed to be no chink in the armor of his superiority, by which he could be attacked. He stood six feet in his stockings, was a shot who lived in the same category as Lord Huntingfield, and a distinguished ornament to the mad Meltonians. He was a man of commanding presence, handsome, dashing, very popular with the ladies. He played whist at the usual stake of £100 the trick, and £1000 the rubber, with an elegant lack of care that spoke worlds about his fortune. He was popular with both sexes, since popularity usually follows success, and he seemed incapable of fear or blunder. He was the man whom Little Tommy hated above all others in the world.

"They had been brought up in adjacent houses, and children are instinctively cruel. In his childhood Sir Marcus had not yet been taught to conceal his feelings, if they were liable to wound. Little Tommy had learned the world's attitude to oddities from the boy's lips. Their parents had encouraged them to play together, with the stupid blindness common to parents in all ages. Tommy had been held up to Marcus as a model of sanctity: Marcus to Tommy, when there was still some faint hope of the latter's growth, as the type of sturdy boyhood. Naturally they had hated each other like poison, and in Tommy's case feared. He was always terrified that Marcus would commit a physical assault upon him. And Marcus, divining the fear by instinct, assumed a horrible ascendancy.

"These physical repulsions are an unpredictable thing. That the dwarf should be afraid of the giant, with the imaginative horror of boyhood, was understandable. But that the giant should have hated the dwarf was a puzzle. Perhaps he hated him for being a model of sanctity; perhaps it was a purely physical repugnance, between creatures of a different species. Whatever the reason, Sir Marcus had become the persecutor of his neighbor.

"All the cruel things that had been said to Little Tommy, and all the practical jokes that had been played upon him, seemed to have originated in the neighboring house. It was the age of practical jokes. Theodore Hook, who perpetrated the Berners Street Hoax, was still alive. You remember the Hoax. A lady resident had earned the animosity of Mr. Hook, and he sat down to write a series of letters. The letters resulted in the simultaneous arrival outside her door of vehicles for coal, furniture, wedding cakes, hearses, sweeps, tradesmen, lawyers, clergymen, fishmongers, brewers, the Lord Mayor, and the Duke of Gloucester. They filled Berners

Street from end to end. The Prince Regent was so delighted
that he presented Mr. Hook a sinecure worth two thousand
pounds a year.

"The joke was cruel, typical of the period. The lady of
Berners Street had to endure it. She, as an unaided individual,
was expected to be able to stand up to all those external
hearses. She was expected to possess the virtues of Sparta:
what we should call 'guts,' and what they called 'bottom.'

"Little Tommy hated references to his stature. Sir Marcus,
whilst they were still on visiting terms, used to talk incessant-
ly about Rutlandshire and the advantages of living at Chis-
wick. He used to send Little Tommy presents of snipe,
whitebait, dwarf gooseberries, and small beer. On the occasion of Tommy's marriage he sent him a doll's house, fitted
with a cradle two inches long, and a letter giving helpfully
intimate advice which can hardly be reproduced in our own
century. The Squire of Bushel flew into a screaming passion
and tried to pick a quarrel with his persecutor. But Sir Marcus
only laughed. It must have been the worst blow. The boisterous mockery, contemptuous and unassailable, rang in the tiny
ears long afterward.

"My great-grandfather entertained as usual in the early autumn of 1838. He was unlike Sir Hercules Lapith, in that he
took the greatest pain not to be provided with instruments
commensurate to his stature. Even his horses were too big for
him, and the four-ten with which he used to shoot was as
large comparatively as Osbaldeston's pigeon gun. He regarded these things as necessary concessions. A normal flintlock would have been nearly beyond his powers to carry.
When, however, it came to the *frills of life*, inessentials like
knives and forks and chairs, he refused to be catered for. He

would climb tediously into the grown-up chair, and there, kneeling surreptitiously on the seat, he would shovel cooked meat into his mouth with a fork that bore comparison with his arm.

"It was horrible to watch him being jolly with his guests, and still more horrible when he felt it incumbent upon him to become boisterous after dinner. To hear him talk about the muscle of Simon Byrne, who had killed the Scottish champion at a boxing match in 1830, was a humiliation to the listener. The poor little creature played the physical game with a dreadful insincerity, like a small boy trying to smoke and swear.

"Little Tommy was anxious to wager on himself. It kept him in the swim, made him feel that he was living the gigantic life successfully. Unfortunately he would never stake upon his peculiarities. If he had betted on his ability to crawl through drain-pipes or ride a Shetland pony forty miles, he would have been betting sensibly and making the best of a bad job. But he refused to be sensible or to admit the job. He once wagered a thousand pounds that he would beat Captain Bentinck in a rowing match from Vauxhall Bridge to Whitehall. He had a special boat constructed, suitable to his own size, but lost the wager lamentably, having been beaten by the waves. On this occasion Sir Marcus Izall sent him a model steamer, five foot long. The jibe entered into his poor little heart; and the Squire of Bushel became secretly unbalanced about competitions. It became a necessity that he should beat a grown man, on his own ground, in order to reinstate his pride. It was not until 1838, at dinner in the early autumn, that the proper opportunity came to hand.

"The great Captain Fosse was staying at Bushel and the

conversation turned on the killing power of the Squire's four-teen. Of course Little Tommy maintained that you could kill more accurately with it than with a larger gun, implying that his reason for not using a twelve-bore was in reality a matter of choice. Captain Fosse objected that the hare, the duck and the pigeon could scarcely come within the category. A head shot at a reasonable distance would account for them, but surely the chances of success were widened by the radius of a twelve-bore. There was a good deal of desperate violence in Tommy's arguments and Fosse was a touchy man. There were plenty of hares at Bushel.

"The upshot was of course a stake.

"I think I ought to mention the wagers of those days. The aphorism that all was fair in love and war was extended into a trinity by the addition of money bets. A wager was fair game for evasion, and the man who won money by observing the letter of the bet but not the spirit was regarded as a legitimate and admirable speculator. Thus Lord Middleton once had a shooting match with a keeper, under the terms of which each had to carry the other's game. The keeper was the better shot and the stronger man. He soon had Lord Middleton stagger-ing across the moors under a load which extinguished all hopes of success: I should say, which would have extin-guished all hopes, if Lord Middleton had not had the inspi-ration to shoot a donkey. So people had to be careful about framing their bets in writing. The stake and conditions were drawn up like a legal document, with a view, from each side, of excluding the evasions of the other party. A wager became a solemn undertaking, carefully and almost legally certified, reported widely and considered with gravity. Sir Marcus Izall, along with the rest of the sporting society, heard of the bet.

"It was impossible that the two men should walk up the game together; for a given hare, equidistant from the two guns, would always be killed by Captain Fosse before Mr. Hance was in a range. The solution that Mr. Hance should walk ten yards in advance of his opponent was objected to by the Captain. So the estate was divided into two halves, at a conference that lasted for four hours, and the competitors drew lots for the halves. It was to be a two-day match, and each was to be allowed to shoot over the territory of the other on the second day. The competitors were to be given the services of a gillie and the supervision of an umpire. Mr. Hance insisted that his own gillie and umpire should walk two hundred yards behind him. He pointed out, reluctantly, that his height gave him a necessary advantage in approaching within range of the quarry: an advantage that would be overthrown by the presence of the other two. After a violent argument Captain Fosse agreed. The match was dated for the following day.

"It was a bright Yorkshire morning, with the edge of winter in the sunny air, and a light wind to rustle the stubble fields: warm in the sun but cold in the shade. Little Tommy had lain awake all night. He was nervous and made a poor business of his first hare, breaking its back near its hind legs. The unpleasantness of killing it whilst it screamed pulled him together, and he shot faultlessly thereafter. The advantage of his height in stalking proved exactly equal to the advantage of Captain Fosse's bore: and they came in at sunset with twenty-seven hares apiece.

"The second day was to be the deciding factor. On the first day Captain Fosse had walked the strip of territory that marched with Sir Marcus Izall's. Now it was Tommy's turn to patrol the frontier. It was for two nights now that he had lain awake, inventing magnificent opportunities, and he was a jumpy shot. On top of that there was the proximity of Sir Marcus, whom he imagined walking stealthily beside him, on the other side of the hedge. Also the hares were thinned.

"Little Tommy plodded through the stubble fields (they reached almost to his thighs) in an anguish of fear and exhaustion. Everything that he wanted to stand for, all the equalities which nature had forbidden him in a whimsy, depended upon the results of his match. He had set not his heart upon it but his life, his self-respect. In an obscure way he would be able to bear even Sir Marcus with equanimity, if he could only win his bet. He would have achieved, asserted his personality, united himself with the spirit of his century. Unfortunately, he had only killed seven hares.

"One of the factors which must be taken into consideration was the length of his stride. He had to take three paces for every one of his opponent's, and these were paces over country where impediments were trebled. If Captain Fosse walked fifteen miles, the dwarf had to walk forty-five. The undertaking was prodigious; the odds against him, and the fatigue, extreme.

"It was at twilight that he came to his last field, with his seven hares in hand and his umpire three hundred yards behind him. He was exhausted, trembling with apprehension for the news of Captain Fosse. The sense of Sir Marcus Izall's proximity was overpowering in the dim light. He reached his last field; and it contained a hare. It was the first hare he had seen for three hours. He was almost too tired to shoot.

"The tiny mannikin stood still for a moment, looking at the hare with a dazed expression, as if it were a foreign thing. Captain Fosse was somewhere in the county, miles away to his left, with an unknown bag. He was an almost certain winner. But not certain. The hares had been thinned.

"An expression of cunning came along into the miniature eye, a chance of possible triumph and a weary anxiety. He began to shake, whether from exhaustion or from fear it was not possible to say. He glanced nervously over his shoulder, and the umpire was at his proper distance, almost invisible in the gathering night. He would see no details. The Squire of Bushel went down on hands and knees, rose cautiously at less than twenty yards. The hare was upright, its ears erect. Little Tommy was torn in an anguish between the desire to go nearer and the fear of disturbing the quarry. He raised his gun with the caution of a flower opening to the sun, hung on the aim until the barrel seemed to point in all directions, and pulled the trigger. It was a horrible breach of etiquette, a sitting shot. The hare fell over.

"Little Tommy found himself running on shaking legs, whose knees swung outward with alarming independence; found himself holding the hare by the ears and looked at it with an astonished eye. Sir Marcus Izall, with several ladies and Sir Bellingham Graham, had popped up behind the neighboring hedge, laughing as if they were going to burst. The hare hung in his hand in a stiff squatting position, with its forelegs doubled up as if it were trying to beg. It was rather badly stuffed.

209

* * *

"Captain Fosse, who had staggered nervously home with thirteen kills, comes out rather well in the sequel to the match. It was he who carried the challenge, with perfect gravity, to the landowner next door. Sir Marcus could laugh it off till he was blue, but the Captain was tenacious. He offered as a concession that the Squire should shoot from horseback, so as to make a better mark.

"Eventually Sir Marcus shrugged his shoulders and asked Sir Bellingham Graham to act as his friend. Sir Bellingham made excuses and refused. He was a good-natured man, faintly ashamed of the practical joke. A local justice of the peace, a man named Farrar, came forward and took his place.

"The arrangements for a duel were as complicated as the arrangements for a bet, but they went forward with a kind of formal celerity. It was arranged that Mr. Hance's dueling pistols should be used, a beautiful pair specially made by Joe Manton some ten years before. They were of normal caliber but extraordinarily light, in order to suit the then hypothetical requirements of the Squire. Sir Marcus consented to this with a curious indifference, although it would put him at the disadvantage of practice. Both men were known to be able to put ten shots on the ace of diamonds at twenty yards.

"When Captain Fosse finally got home, late that night, he found the Squire in bed, but waking. He told him that the matter would have to be settled next morning at six o'clock, on the sands near Scarborough. It was the earliest moment at which the light could be expected to be perfect, and it would entail a journey of two hours by coach, before dawn.

"The miniature Squire got out of bed at once, and spent the night putting his affairs in order, with the assistance of the Captain. It was a lengthy job, particularly as the Squire's mind was not in the work.

"He was not afraid. Far from it, he burned with a rapture of enthusiasm that made him a troublesome partner at making wills. It was exactly what he wanted, the very thing to solve his troubles in a flash. He gloated on the figure of speech 'in a flash,' he remarked to the laboring Captain, à propos of nothing at all. But the Captain recognized a part of the allusion, saw the mental flame stabbing the darkness, and smelled powder.

"Little Tommy was beside himself with excitement. He tried to behave with dignity and to give an undivided attention to his estate, but all the time he was thinking of the flash. The little Manton would nestle in his hand, as light as if it had been baked by a French cook, and he would press the trigger and the flash would leap out of the noise. The black and smelly powder would hang for a moment, obscuring the crumbling figure of Sir Marcus, and as the figure crumbled his own troubles would vanish with the smoke. It would make up for the match at hare-shooting even. He forgot all resentment toward Sir Marcus. It never crossed his mind that he might himself be killed.

"You see, the duel had turned out to be a way of meeting the giant race, arm against arm, and of establishing his equality on common ground. It was the perfect way. His blundering previous attempts to justify his early Victorian body, with rowing of races and shooting of hares, had been fumbling only toward the great solution. When he had killed a man of normal stature, actually raped him of his life under refereed conditions, he might well be able to boast himself the equal of the race. Sir Marcus would be his stepping-stone to equality, and Little Tommy forgave him for that reason; though he was faintly glad that it was Sir Marcus he was going to kill and not somebody else.

"Just before they started, at four o'clock, he remembered his last duty. He went into his wife's bedroom and woke her up.

" 'Philadelphia,' he said, 'I am going after the duck.'

" 'Why tell me?' inquired Mrs. Hance.

" 'I was thinking that you might like to know,' said the Squire awkwardly. Then, taking one of her fingers in his small fist, he kissed her clumsily on the knuckles. He went down to the coaches in the dark.

"The topic of conversation between Bushel and Scarborough was a continuous interrogatory conducted by the Squire on the subject of the Osbaldeston–Bentinck affair. Was it true that one or both of the pistols had not been loaded with ball? Had he Captain Fosse's solemn assurance that nothing of that sort would be allowed to happen on the present occasion? Was Farrar absolutely to be trusted? Might he load the pistols himself? Would the principals start with their backs to one another?

"On this point the Captain had something to say. No, the principals would not start back to back. It had been arranged that Mr. Hance should fire from horseback, and the turning of his horse would put him at a disadvantage. The principals would stand facing one another, but they would be required by the judge to hold their pistols at their sides and to look at him. The pistols would not be cocked. The judge was instructed to say two words, 'Ready? Fire!' Until he said the second word neither of the protagonists was to look away from the judge or to raise or cock his pistol.

"Little Tommy seemed scarcely to be listening. Was it true, he inquired, that Colonel Anson had stopped Mr. Osbaldeston at the critical moment and then given Lord George Bentinck the word to fire when the former was off his guard? Was the judge in the present instance to be absolutely depended upon? It was a matter of the first importance.

"They walked over the dunes in the early light, plowing through the dry heavy powder of the sand, skirting the prickly grasses which bound the barriers together against the sea. There was a nip in the air. One of the coach horses was unharnessed and led down to the beach. Sir Marcus had not arrived.

"Waiting is usually the worst part of anything that we have to suffer. On the beach there was nothing to do. If the idea of being killed had crossed my great-grandfather's mind he might have spent the next half-hour in torment. On the contrary, he was as happy as a sandboy. The solution of his troubles had been sprung upon him so beautifully, and without the necessity of effort on his part, that he never doubted for a moment. Sir Marcus was sure to come, sure to be killed. Little Tommy spent the time throwing pebbles at the seagulls, as if there was nothing else that mattered in the world.

"Sir Marcus arrived. He advanced with the surgeon, Mr. Farrar and the judge, all four dressed in long black cloaks. Sir Marcus had a black neckerchief as well, so that there was no white showing on his person. He was pale but perfectly controlled, and was seen to be laughing heartily at a private joke. The judge approached Captain Fosse, asking whether it

213

might not be possible to settle the affair without bloodshed at the last moment. Captain Fosse had been instructed to refuse. Sir Marcus and Mr. Farrar then most irregularly approached the Squire and suggested that the duel should be fought with squirts. They produced a brace of them and offered to squirt their opponent. Captain Fosse angrily interposed.

"Everything began to pass in a kind of dream, smoothly and without feeling. Mr. Hance mounted the coach horse, the distances were paced, the pistols loaded by the judge and inspected by both seconds. Sir Marcus and Mr. Hance avoided each other's eyes. It must have been at this time that the former realized his position. His last taunt had been instinctive, his hopes of bluffing it out, of seeing the catastrophe averted in time by some external agency, were vain; and he was a proud man. He waited, looking at the sand.

"For Mr. Hance the world went into slow motion. They faced the judge obediently, seeing behind him the white arrested flakes of the gulls and the ground mist of September. The judge had a small wart beside his nose. Little Tommy sat sideways on his horse, barebacked, looking at the wart. The backbone of the horse was hard.

"The judge spoke distinctly, using the expected formula. The pistol rose with a great effort, seeming to lug itself upward against pressure, like a man walking through the sea. It cocked as it rose. The horse, startled by the movement, began to shy. The pistol, divining the shy before it started, moved of its own volition toward the right. It produced a mushroom of black smoke: no flash: and some time afterward a loud report.

214

"The smoke had no effect upon Sir Marcus. The noise seemed to make him start.

"Mr. Hance peered at him through the powder, moving his head slightly to one side like an obstructed member of the audience trying to see better at the cinema. The baronet's face was the same color as the sand, and had a mixed expression of defiance and surprise. He remained upright, with his pistol at his side.

"Mr. Hance opened his mouth.

"Sir Marcus Izall began to look fatigued. He raised his pistol well away from the body, away from the seconds, away from the Squire. When it was pointing straight up into the air he pulled the trigger. Then, as if the second explosion had been too much for him, he fell flat on his back.

"Little Tommy saw it for the first time in his second's face. They had all run to Sir Marcus. The blood, squirting over the fine sand, had rolled itself into gritty pellets that looked odd. Little Tommy had stayed on his horse.

"They came back to him at last, and he read the message in a side glance, an evasion of the unhappy Captain's eyes. They were eyes of hostility and secret shame. Sir Marcus Izall was a dead giant. My great-grandfather was a broken dwarf, who had lost his status after all.

"He ought to have thought of it before. If Goliath had killed David he would have been the prototype of cads. It had been impossible for the bigger man even to take an aim."

A Link with Petulengro

On December 25, 1836, a determined little armful of femininity, aged seventeen, had her breakfast at nine o'clock. She usually woke up half an hour or an hour before she got out of bed, and took thirty minutes to dress, so we may assume that those bright eyes opened on that rather distant Christmas morning at about 7:30. This was a bit late, for her. The reason was that she had "stayed up" on Christmas Eve until eleven o'clock.

After breakfast she, with her mother and her governess, read morning prayers. Then she arranged her new drawings.

In the early days of the nineteenth century people did not give each other their presents on Christmas Day. They gave them on Christmas Eve, and with a different ritual from our modern one. The Christmas trees were invented already, but, instead of stockings there were "tables." In all the rooms of the big country house inhabited by our heroine, which was near Esher, on the Portsmouth Road, there had been a bustle on December 24, as the tables had been arranged with secrecy and excitement: one for Mamma, one for the governess and one for the busy maiden. At precisely six o'clock on the eve of the festival, Mamma had summoned everybody to visit their tables in the gallery and to collect their presents. It had been pretty in the snowy evening, with the two lighted fir-trees, hung with sugar ornaments, and the tables groaning with small gifts.

On the girl's table there had been, so her Diary tells us, "2 lovely little Dresden china figures, 2 pair of lovely little chased gold buttons, a small lovely button with an angel's head which she [the governess] used to wear herself, and a pretty music book." All these were from the governess.

Her mother had given her "a beautiful massive gold buckle in the shape of two serpents; a lovely little delicate gold chain with a turquoise-clasp; a lovely coloured sketch of dearest Aunt Louise by Partridge, copied from the picture he brought, and so like her; 3 beautiful drawings by Munn, one lovely sea view by Purser, and one beautiful cattle piece by Cooper (all coloured), 3 prints, a book called *Finden's Tableaux, Heath's Picturesque Annual for 1837;* both these very pretty; *Friendship's Offering*, and *The English Annual for 1837, The Holy Land*, illustrated beautifully, two handkerchiefs, a very pretty black satin apron trimmed with red velvet, and two almanacks."

It was because of all these excitements that she had stayed up late, and risen late on Christmas Day, and it was these brand-new drawings which she was arranging after morning prayers.

The mansion in which she was arranging them had been built by Sir John Vanbrugh and bought by the Duke of Newcastle. Later, it had belonged to the famous Lord Clive. William Kent and Capability Brown had laid out its estate—now broken up for building—and, on the morning in question, the castellated prospect tower which stood on a mount near the house was lustered with icicles like a chandelier.

218

A Link with Petulengro

*   *   *

In a shallow dingle outside the park on the Portsmouth Road there was a gipsy camp.

Looking like the very tattered hood of a disreputable double perambulator, and surrounded with the usual mysterious litter of the Romanies—old bottles, bits of metal, cast-off clothing and pieces of cloth tied in the hedgerows, presumably as secret signs to later comers—the single tent stood in the Surrey landscape like a drunk tramp at a white wedding.

For it was still snowing. It had been a bitter night and it was a bitter morning. In the blanched, gelid, crunching cleanness, the grubby and threadbare untidiness of the tarpaulin and bent sticks looked sinister. The fresh snow and the squalor of odds-and-ends were at a contrast.

Outside the tent, squatting on his hunkers, was Mr. Cooper, the paterfamilias of the tribe, who was doing something obscure in the vicinity of the wood fire. The blue smoke went up straight, into the *poilu* sky. Perhaps he was skinning a poached hare; perhaps he was mending a kettle; perhaps he was whittling a stick with which to thrash his wife or his grandmother; perhaps he was making a trap or a roasting-spit or something tricky to do with horses. A melancholy but likely looking gelding, with fired legs, stood in the offing. The swift, furtive, efficient, secret movements of Mr. Cooper made it impossible to determine what he was at. He was a spare, thinly clad, lithe specimen, with flashing teeth, and he had a peacock feather in his hat.

Aunt Sarah, squatting opposite the head of the household, was smoking twist in a broken clay pipe, while she querulously complained about the frost. She wore a poke bonnet.

219

Outside the low entrance of the tent, which looked not unlike a diminutive Nissen hut constructed out of broken umbrellas, there stood a creature of pure wonder. She was wearing a straw hat, such as harvesters used to wear in the days of Rowlandson, a plaid shawl, a skirt, and little else. Amber-colored, dark-haired, nut-eyed, slender, round, straight, strong, soft, smooth, twenty years old, with classic features, all fire, she stood erect at the tent mouth, with a baby at her neat, bare breast. The baby's eyes, like prunes, slipped vaguely about the universe in a fat, brown face, meditating milk. They were soup-colored searchlights, out of focus.

A greyhound, with head and tail drooping in the beautiful yet hangdog sickle of its variety, stood shivering in the snow, with slim, grim jaws pondering rabbits.

Who were these people? In 1836, George Borrow was selling the Bible in Spain. Jasper Petulengro's father and mother had been transported, *bitchadey parodel*, and were dead, while Jasper himself must have been nearing forty. Perhaps the Coopers were related to the mother-in-law of Borrow's Pharaoh, to that fearsome old lady whose battle-cry was, "My name is Herne, and I comes of the hairy ones!" At all events, since most gipsies of the period knew each other, they may have been personally acquainted with many of the characters in *Lavengro*. They might have met the Flaming Tinman himself, and might even have been intimidated by Isopel Berners, who had once been taught to conjugate "I love" in Armenian.

At the moment they were dealing in higher game than even the Pharaoh had aspired to—though it has to be admitted that the latter, in old age, was rumored, in *Wild Wales*, to have been made a Justice of the Peace and Deputy Ranger of Windsor Park.

The official story of the family, as it had been presented to our heroine, was that the bronzed Venus with the baby was Mrs. Cooper, that she had given birth to this infant about three weeks ago in the encampment, and that all were desperately in need of fuel and nourishment. Mr. Cooper and family were making a point of not knowing who was the tenant of the house near which they had settled down, and, to be candid, the real tenant of the house, our heroine, was making rather a point of not knowing who she was likely to be herself.

It must have been with many Borrovian cries of "*Shoon, thimble-engro, avella, gorgio*" ["Listen, thimble-rigger, here comes a non-gipsy"] or of "*Dosta, tiny tawny*" ["Enough, little one"] or of *morts, mards* and *mumpings* [women, husbands and vagabonds] that the watchful dependents of Mr. Cooper cautioned one another to readiness as a reluctant procession arrived upon the scene.

Three footmen in full livery, in scarlet coats, gold lace, buckskin breeches and trembling calves, minced disdainfully and miserably through the snow. They bore with them, like the three Wise Men of Orient, gifts of fuel, soup and covering. They were Cockneys, and they thought that they knew all about Mr. Cooper: their silk stockings were not only soaked but also frozen: they dumped the hateful presents without ceremony and withdrew, stepping high because of the snow, with various Sam-Weller-like remarks, in which the "v" was substituted for the "w."

If there was tension in the gipsy camp there was an equal
excitement at the Great House.

What, what was the right thing to do with vagabonds? The
Governess said that it was very wrong indeed to encourage
people who would not work for themselves. It was, she said,
to encourage destitution. The more you gave to weak people,
because they were weak, the more you encouraged them to
be helpless. She was an enduring, bony woman, with an aqui-
line or anteater nose and a faithful heart. All the time that she
was saying this, she was looking through an old portmanteau
in which she believed that there was a worsted knit jacket
which would do for the baby.

Mamma said, "Yes," but in her station it was one's duty to
assist the poor. The question was, how much? She was only
too willing to send blankets, but how many blankets? How
many blankets did one have on a bed?

Our heroine suggested "Eight?"

"No, no, there are never more than four."

"What is a blanket?"

"It is the hairy one on the top, I believe, instead of the
counterpane."

"But then; there is only one?"

"My love, I do not know how many there are. Perhaps
only one."

"It would have to be washed?"

"Then two," said our heroine. "One to use and one to
wash. Would that be encouraging the poor?"

Nobody seemed to know anything about this.

"Two," she said.

Her rather blowsy mother explained defensively: "I have sent soup and fuel, dear. I am sure Sir John would have told us what to do."

It was now two o'clock, and it was time for the expedition to set forth. There were in the carriage: our heroine; her half-sister, Victoire, and the Governess. The broth and the fuel and two blankets—which now seemed to these innocent creatures exactly the right number—had been ordered in advance. The Governess had found the worsted jacket. Our heroine held, clutched in a plump, chilly paw, the sum of one guinea. It might have been one penny for all she could distinguish between the coins of the realm.

The Coopers were ready for their visitors.

As the high wheels of the carriage crunched into the snow of the camp, the patriarchal troop, like a tableau of Bethlehem, turned out.

Mr. Cooper, with many cringings, let down the step of the carriage.

He said: "Great health to you, kind lady."

Our heroine, who was direct, began with: "How is the baby?"

"The *chabo* is doing well, high maiden."

"And how is the mother?"

"By your kindness, Princess of Beauty, the mother is well also."

The two groups confronted each other, as the Kings of the East had confronted the maternal scene in a manger, and there was, even in the present scene, a sort of awe on both sides. From the viewpoint of the nomad mother, there was real awe for the greatness of her visitors, combined with a defiance, a wild, defensive den-feeling, as of the tigress with her cub. This was combined with the cunning of the vixen and with the beauty of Egypt—the beauty of a royal lady whom Antony had once addressed by her title as "Egypt." There was also the pride of motherhood.

It was for this motherhood that our heroine, on her part, felt awe and envy, a touch of hero worship. To be so beautiful, so brown, so brave, so free, so fulfilled with mystery! She was well aware of her own importance, though she would not admit it, yet here was an importance of a different sort, higher at present than her maiden one. She looked upon the gipsy *mort* with a timidity and tender respect and longing. She held out a finger toward the baby.

With a gesture which was at once saucy and bashful, the mother turned back her shawl still further to offer the small starfish of a hand, which closed upon the finger. The baby's mouth began to bubble. Mr. Cooper watched disdainfully, while the ladies cooed. Women, he thought: the *gorgios* were worse than his own!

But the expedition had come with a second object, apart from baby-worship. The three ladies in the carriage had been frequently assured by Sir John Conroy that fortune-telling was flummery. They had agreed respectfully that it was not only flummery, but also wicked, since it had been expressly forbidden in the Bible. And yes, they knew quite well that the whole business was nonsense. So, being feminine, they had come to have their fortunes told, and had agreed to keep it a secret, particularly from Sir John.

The last of them to show her hand was our heroine. With what conjectures, with what trepidation, and with what secret hopes and yet with what imperious decision she held it out! It was ringless, white, smooth, short-fingered, tapered, with dimples instead of knuckles.

Mr. Cooper's *chie*, the Venus of this yuletide scene, had of course been schooled by Mr. Cooper with the exact words of her royal prophecy, her *dukkeripen*. All hoped for at least a *bull* [five shillings].

But some flash had passed between the eyes of the two young ones—the mother and the maiden—some electricity of recognition and affection, by which each one loved the other, and respected her heart's hopes, and knew why. With a clash of bangles, without disturbing the baby in the shawl, with a sweep of the tattered skirt and a swift, controlled obeisance, the dimpled hand was first pressed to the Brow of Egypt, and then the brow itself, with exquisite grace, had sunk to the level of the carriage step, where it rested in a moment of homage upon the cross-gartered, satin slipper of the virgin blanket-bearer.

No word was spoken. The moment was held for one heart-beat. Then all, as if by one accord, unfroze themselves. The Venus rose, the warm guinea was pressed into the starfish hand, which clutched it, Mr. Cooper swept off his peacock hat, and the coachman, without instructions, whipped up his shining, steaming clinking horses through the snow.

That Christmas evening, before she went to bed, our seven-teen-year-old sister of charity remembered to write her diary. "I cannot say how happy I am," she wrote, "that these poor

225

creatures are assisted, for they are such a nice set of gipsies, so quiet, so affectionate to one another, so discreet, not at all forward or importunate, and *so* grateful; so unlike the gossiping, fortune-telling race-gipsies; and this is such a peculiar and touching case. Their being assisted makes me quite merry and happy to-day, for yesterday night when I was safe and happy at home in that cold night and to-day when it snowed so and everything looked white, I felt quite unhappy and grieved to think that our poor gipsy friends should perish and shiver for want; and now to-day I shall go to bed happy, knowing they are better off and more comfortable . . ."

She did go to bed, in quite a glow of achievement, and, as usual, was asleep almost before her head had touched the pillow. It was only at St. Leonard's-on-Sea that she used to sleep badly, on account of the moaning of the sea. But before she dozed away in her snug nest, by the cozy, saffron light of the coal fire which shone on the toilet table ("white muslin cover over pink, and all my silver things standing on it with a fine new looking-glass)," the colors and the music and the aspirations of a debutante may have whirled together briefly through the shining head, in its tight curl-papers. She may have thought of her mother's "dear little paroquet of a green colour with a pale brown head, and so very tame that Mamma took it on her finger and it would hardly leave her. It is not so remarkable for its fine plumage than for its great tameness. It talks also, the man says."

If she thought of the paroquet, she would have thought also of her own "most delightful *Lory*, which is so tame that it remains on your hand, and you may put your finger into its beak, or do anything with it, without its even attempting to bite." It was "larger than Mamma's grey parrot, and has a most beautiful plumage; it is scarlet, blue, brown, yellow and purple."

If it was in the form of music that her dreams came upon her, it will have been the music of Rossini, Bellini, Donizetti and others of the Italian school admired by her adored music-master, Lablache—whose volubility of tongue was wonderful; "he can sing such quantities of words and at such a rate!" She was genuinely fond of music, though with no great taste in it. Handel, for instance, she found "very heavy and tiresome."

But if she sank into dreams with gentle thoughts of the affections, who can say what the dreams would be at seventeen? Perhaps they were of her precious governess, her "best and truest friend," whom she had known "for nearly seventeen years and I trust I shall have for thirty or forty and *many* more!" Perhaps they were of M. Lablache himself, that nice, good-natured, good-humored, patient and excellent master, who was "so merry too." Perhaps they were of her various cousins, whom she might have been expected to marry. "Dearly as I love Ferdinand, and also good Augustus, I love Ernest and Albert *more* than them, oh yes, MUCH *more*." It is as likely that her last thoughts may have been for her pony *Rosa* ("SWEET LITTLE ROSY went BEAUTIFULLY!"), or for her King Charles spaniel, darling *Dashy*. Most likely of all, her dreams may have been of the gipsies, her own gipsies, "to *my* feeling, the chief ornament of the Portsmouth Road . . . they are happy and grateful and we have done them some good. The place and spot may be forgotten, but the gipsy family Cooper will *never* be obliterated from my memory!"

They never were. In later life she was always partial to the

Romanies, as witness the rumor that she had made Petulen-gro the Deputy Ranger of Windsor Park. Nor was the *duk-kerin* of that dusky sybil who had kissed her hand at all a bad one. It was only three months after this happy and exciting Christmas in 1836 that the Archbishop of Canterbury woke our armful up at six o'clock in the morning, to tell her that she was Queen Victoria.